It was all t *lying on that bed with Ava beside him.*

He could still recall the feel of her supple muscles and soft curves.

As if recognizing his thoughts, she took a step back. "No." Her voice was firm. But in her expression he saw a reflection of the desire he was trying desperately to stem in himself. "We aren't going to make the same mistake twice."

"That's good to hear." His mind splintered into dueling parts: logic and temptation. His hand reached out, as if devoid of conscious decision, and cupped her jaw.

Her hand came up as if to push his away. Lingered to stroke. "You don't trust me," she said.

The skin beneath her ear was baby soft. When he brushed his fingertips over it she shuddered.

"I can't."

"So why should I trust you?"

He replaced his hand with his lips, tracing her delicate jawline with a string of whisper-soft kisses. "You shouldn't."

Dear Reader,

When I see newspaper accounts of a daring rescue mounted by special tactical teams, I always find myself wondering about the qualities of the men and women drawn to that sort of work. But none are more mysterious to me than the role of sniper.

The precision marksmen are usually the most seasoned members of the SWAT team. They are the first ones called to a hostage situation, and the last ones to leave. Because of their vantage point, they also impart intelligence to the individuals in the command center. All must be prepared to make split-second, life-and-death decisions in volatile and rapidly evolving situations.

Ava Carter is a sniper. She's also a cop, a mother and a woman with a secret she's gone to great lengths to hide. But when she agrees to team up with Cael McCabe, she quickly discovers that the danger of the job at hand is the least of the perils she'll encounter. The riskiest will be deciding whether she can trust the man who threatens her career…and her heart.

I hope you enjoy Ava and Cael's story as much as I enjoyed writing it!

All the best,

Kylie Brant

KYLIE BRANT

Terms of Attraction

Silhouette®
Romantic
SUSPENSE

SILHOUETTE BOOKS

Recycling programs for this product may not exist in your area.

ISBN-13: 978-0-373-27639-4

TERMS OF ATTRACTION

Copyright © 2009 by Kimberly Bahnsen

Visit Silhouette Books at www.eHarlequin.com

Printed in U.S.A.

Books by Kylie Brant

Silhouette Romantic Suspense

McLain's Law #528
Rancher's Choice #552
An Irresistible Man #622
Guarding Raine #693
Bringing Benjy Home #735
Friday's Child #862
Undercover Lover #882
Heartbreak Ranch #910
Falling Hard and Fast #959
Undercover Bride #1022
†*Hard To Handle* #1108
Born in Secret #1112
†*Hard To Resist* #1119
†*Hard To Tame* #1125
**Alias Smith
 and Jones #1196

**Entrapment* #1221
**Truth or Lies* #1238
**Dangerous Deception* #1306
In Sight of the Enemy #1323
Close to the Edge #1341
The Business of Strangers #1366
The Last Warrior #1437
††*Terms of Surrender* #1533
††*Terms of Engagement* #1545
††*Terms of Attraction* #1569

*The Sullivan Brothers
†Charmed and Dangerous
**The Tremaine Tradition
††Alpha Squad

KYLIE BRANT

is a bestselling, award-winning author of twenty-five novels for Silhouette Romantic Suspense. When she's not dreaming up stories of romance and suspense, she works as a teacher for learning-disabled elementary students.

Kylie invites readers to check out her Web site at www.kyliebrant.com for news, backlist and information about upcoming releases. She can be contacted by e-mail at kyliebrant@hotmail.com.

For Keaden, my newest grandson,
who already owns a piece of my heart.

Acknowledgments

As always, a huge thank-you to Kyle Hiller, Captain, Special Response Team, for your generous assistance. I'm awed by both your knowledge and your dedication to duty!

Chapter 1

Ava Carter lay motionless atop the gravel and tar flat roof squinting through the Nightforce scope of the Remington 700 rifle. She'd been in position for nearly four hours; under a "weapons tight" command for two. If all went according to plan, the subject would be on his way—in one piece—in less than fifteen minutes.

The rheumy late February sun labored to pierce the light cloud cover, and there was small blessing in that. Temperatures still hovered in the high sixties. And even without direct sunlight she could feel a thin trickle of perspiration snaking down her back beneath the LBV vest.

The breeze kissing her cheek seemed to have gotten a little stronger. "Check the wind meter again."

Her spotter, Steve Banes, held up the pocket calibrator. "Six point two four miles per hour."

Ava adjusted the dope of her rifle slightly. Steve picked

up his high-powered binoculars again and spoke into the Motorola radio. "Side three, opening three. No movement."

She reached for her own set of binoculars. Through them she could clearly see the black RV that served as the SWAT command center parked a hundred yards from the civic center. She could make out the figure of a man through one of the windows, hunched over a computer.

Her gaze passed over the RV to scan the area. She and Steve were positioned on top of a building across the road about eight hundred yards from the civic center. The building they were observing was circular, with an oddly pitched roof that was supposed to enhance the acoustics inside. Beneath the overhang were narrow windows encircling the building.

The inner perimeter seemed secure. The interested public was still inside listening to Antonio de la Reyes. But it was his detractors that were cause for concern.

From this angle she could only see a corner of the group of protesters and media vans secured behind the outer perimeter in front of the civic center. There were still a few signs waving, but a majority of the picketers had wisely decided to save their strength for when de la Reyes made his exit.

Hopefully once they figured out he wasn't coming out the front, de la Reyes would be on his way to the airport. Out of Metro City. Out of California and back to his small South American country of San Baltes.

Good riddance.

It wasn't his politics Ava objected to, though his eloquent arguments for opening the borders of America didn't resonate for her. It was the target he presented. In the last week alone, as he'd traveled the country, he'd received almost a dozen death threats. Pretty unpopular for a visiting dignitary. She'd heard there was a small rebel contingent in his own country that was just as anxious to see him dead.

She was only anxious to see him gone.

"What's he even doing here?" grumbled Banes. He was a

large man, heavily muscled. His shaved head was the color of her morning double mocha latte and glistened with sweat.

"He has relatives here, I think I heard. His mother lived in Metro City until the seventies."

Banes's droopy dark mustache twitched in what might have been a smirk. "Like you'd remember anything about the seventies."

"Just enough to know seventy-seven was a very good year." Ava continued to scan the area. They'd had this conversation often enough in the past that she could participate without thinking. Banes had a good fifteen years on her, and he liked to rib her about his experience. He'd been on SWAT ten years longer than she had. He was a damn good marksman, ranking second in the Metro City PD, fourth in the state.

Ava ranked first in both.

"Have you ever been inside?"

She nodded. "Took my son to a concert there once. It's pretty nice. All the seats have a good view of the stage." It must have been about three years ago, when Alex was twelve, before he became afflicted with that weird teenage parental anathema. At fifteen he could barely be convinced to be seen with her at the mall.

The radio crackled. "De la Reyes has left the stage. Subject will be exiting from side three, opening one in the next two minutes."

Ava kept the binoculars raised. De la Reyes's white limo approached slowly and rolled to a stop by the curb. It would have been checked thoroughly before being allowed through the inner perimeter. Security inside the building would be directing the public out the front. Officers would keep the people from circling around to the back entrance. Everything was working according to plan.

She was about to lower the binoculars when something caught her eye. A glint in one of the civic center's upper windows. In the next instant it had disappeared. "Do you see anything up there?"

Banes trained his binoculars in the area she was pointing to. "Nope."

"Must have been the sun," she muttered. But there was very little sunlight today. Which made it more likely she'd seen a reflection of some sort. But of what?

"Wait." She and Banes spoke simultaneously. She went on. "You see it, too, right? What is that?"

Both of them stared for long moments through their binoculars. A chill broke out over Ava's skin as comprehension slammed into her. "It's a scope."

Banes grabbed the radio. "We've got a reflection in side three, window seven. Looks like it could be from a rifle scope."

"Cold Shot in position?" came the answer.

"Affirmative."

"Weapons tight. We'll send someone inside to check it out."

Ava set down the binoculars and peered through the Nightforce scope of her Remington. She made the minute adjustments necessary to focus on the window in question. "I see the barrel," she reported quietly. A familiar deadly calm settled over her. "Can you get another angle and make it out?"

Steve belly-crawled several yards away and took another look through the binoculars. As an answer, he spoke through the radio. "We've got a weapon sighted and verified. Side three, window seven."

The radio crackled. "Keep target inside. We've got a sighting."

She heard the voice as if from a distance. Ava's entire system had slowed. Breathing. Nerves. Heart rate. Everything was focused on the individual on the other end of that rifle across the road. The best shot would be to shoot perpendicular from the window. But she didn't have time to change position. Shooting at an angle meant firing two shots. The first to break the glass and the second to hit the target.

"What the hell?" muttered Banes as the back door entrance opened. Ava recognized de la Reyes surrounded by his private contingent of security and three tactical officers hurrying toward the steps.

"Weapons loose. Engage, engage."

She was dimly aware of the group surrounding de la Reyes halting. Retreating toward the civic center. Her finger squeezed the trigger and fired twice in quick succession through the target window. Nearly simultaneously an answering shot sounded and one of the bodies on the steps crumpled.

Ava gave her watch a surreptitious look and sighed mentally. If this was going to drag on much longer she'd need to excuse herself and text Alex. He'd be getting out of basketball practice soon and might need to catch a different ride home.

The debriefing was going more slowly than usual. But then nothing about this incident had proven normal yet.

The door to the conference room opened and Chief of Police Carl Sanders entered, flanked by his deputy chief, Robert Grey. They were followed by Antonio de la Reyes and a few men she remembered from his security contingent.

There was a scraping of chairs as a few of the SWAT officers made room at the long table. Ava sat still as the new-comers stared her way, feeling like an insect on a pin.

"There she is, gentlemen. The officer of the hour."

There was little doubt about whom Sanders was referring to. Ava was the only woman in the room. Without looking away from her, de la Reyes circled the table to come to a halt before her.

"Ms. Carter," he said in melodic fluent English. "I am in your debt."

Since he'd taken her hand and looked to be in no hurry to free it, Ava rose, ill at ease. "I'm glad it worked out."

He looked more like a movie star than a politician. He was no taller than she, about five nine, with glossy dark hair and soulful brown eyes. But she recognized the tailor-fitted suit he wore and the designer shoes. His country's impoverishment didn't extend to this man.

"It worked out, as you say, for all but your fellow officer." Finally de la Reyes released her hand and glanced back at Sanders. "But I am told the man is well."

Sanders nodded, his craggy face grim. "Sergeant Talbot was saved by his vest. He'll be sore for a few days, but he's already been released from the hospital."

There was a collective murmur of relief from the room's occupants.

De la Reyes went to sit in a nearby free chair and Ava sank into her own with a sense of reprieve. She'd never learned to enjoy the spotlight.

Sanders pulled out a chair. "The would-be assassin has been identified."

"His name is Pedro Cabrerra." Ava recognized the man passing out sheets as head of the American company providing de la Reyes security while in the country. He was the sort of man who left an impression.

A shade under six feet, he had a commanding presence, even in a roomful of cops. His streaked blond hair bordered on shaggy, his pale green gaze hawklike. His face was tanned as a surfer's and his body looked broad and rock hewn beneath his suit. Unlike de la Reyes, whose expensive clothes gilded his sophisticated appearance, this man's suit only served to highlight what he was beneath it. A warrior. No amount of gloss or polish could ever mask his rough edges.

"I am sorry." De la Reyes lifted a hand to indicate the man passing out Cabrerra's likeness. "Cael McCabe. He owns the security company I hired shortly before I came to the States."

McCabe was the only one to remain standing. And he didn't so much pace the room as prowl. "Cabrerra was a trusted member of Senor de la Reyes's private security detail who traveled with him from San Baltes."

Kylie Brant   13

"He is…was," de la Reyes corrected himself, "my first cousin. Our fathers are brothers."

Ava saw the grief in the man's eyes and felt a moment of sympathy. Bad enough for complete strangers to want you dead. But when your own family went gunning for you…that transcended politics. It didn't get any more personal.

"Cabrerra was part of the security contingent to go through the civic center prior to Antonio's appearance there."

"But how the hell did he smuggle in a weapon?" Chief Sanders demanded. "Rifle, scope, tripod…he didn't carry all that equipment in when he was helping with the security sweep."

"He probably went in the night before," McCabe responded. There was the slightest hint of Georgia in his voice. He might have lost the drawl, but the rounded vowels gave him away. "The windows aren't wired to the alarm system. No reason to be. They're too narrow for a person to enter through. He must have rappelled up the side of the building with the equipment in a bag over his shoulder. We found a window with the lock drilled out. All he had to do then was open the window, drop the bag inside and close it again. He just had to make sure he was first in the building the next morning so he could choose the section he was going to 'secure.' Stash the equipment until he needed it."

"Those windows all open onto hallways that circle the top of the building," SWAT commander Harv Mendel observed.

McCabe nodded. "He probably locked the doors leading to the seating. Hard to blend in if he'd tried to take out Antonio during his speech. But leaving the building…he could have arrived on-scene moments later and no one would have suspected him. Better yet, everyone would have figured it was one of the nut jobs that have been issuing threats. Not one of his own countrymen."

The mood in the room went grim. "No offense, Senor de la Reyes…" The chief stumbled a bit over the pronunciation. "But he had five days and as many cities to act before you stopped in Metro City. What was he waiting for?"

"This I do not know."

"'I can guess." McCabe shoved his hands in the pockets of his dark suit jacket, the motion pulling the fabric tight across his shoulders. "He figured this was his best chance to get away with it. He counted on a smaller police force. Less experienced security." He sent a slight smile at Ava. "He figured wrong."

The effect of that smile sent a frisson clear down her spine. Nerve endings quivered in response. Long-dormant hormones stirred. Ava straightened in her chair and stared back at McCabe, fighting for an impassive expression. There wasn't a man alive who could affect her with just a look. Few who could affect her *at all*. A man that potent wasn't just one to be wary of.

He was downright lethal.

"Ms. Carter."

She half turned, her posture wary. Cael quickened his stride to catch up with her and wondered, not for the first time, what it was about the woman that drew this visceral immediate response. She was attractive, with hair and eyes so dark she could pass for a countrywoman of de la Reyes, if it weren't for her pale skin. But he didn't react to every attractive female he saw, especially on a job.

"What is it, McCabe?"

One corner of his mouth kicked up at the impatience in her tone. Her voice was a low alto, slightly raspy. Every time he heard it he thought of sex. Hot and sweaty and exhausting.

"If you've got a few minutes, I'd like to buy you a drink." He was close enough to see the mask slide over her expression, and found himself intrigued yet again. Maybe she was used to men hitting on her and had developed an instant defense. He wasn't hitting on her, but he'd be lying if he said the thought hadn't occurred to him.

"Sorry. I need to get home." There was no trace of regret in her voice. She pushed open the door of the Metro City Police Headquarters and jogged down the steps.

"I'll walk you to your car, then." And it satisfied something inside him to intercept her sidewise glance, half irritated and half questioning. But she made no effort at conversation, clearly leaving that up to him.

He shoved his hands in his suit pockets and fleetingly wondered how long it would be before he could change into something that didn't feel like a straitjacket. "So. Good shooting today. Were you lucky or are you that good?"

"I'm that good," she said without a hint of modesty. And because it was no more than he'd heard, he nodded.

"Cold Shot. That's your call sign, right? From what I hear, it's well earned." They stepped into the parking lot. "Who spotted the shooter first?"

"I work with a partner. He was in the conference room. Steve Banes."

And that, he noted, didn't answer the question. "Banes told your chief that you noticed it first." She didn't respond and he took that as an affirmative. So she wasn't quick to take credit, a team player. Both facts only cemented his earlier decision. "I'd like to offer you a job."

The hitch in her gait was the only sign he'd surprised her. "No." Then after a pause that made it clear it was an afterthought, she added, "Thanks."

"Haven't heard my offer yet." He figured which was her car before she stopped in front of it. A Pontiac, seven or eight years old, and showing its age. "My company, Global Security, specializes in a full array of security solutions. I'm always looking to hire qualified individuals. Your performance today was impressive." Even more impressive had been what Chief Sanders had to say about Carter's experience. He was still trying to square her reputation with the tall, lithe woman beside him who'd look more at home on a runway than in SWAT gear.

She clicked the automatic opener on the car, then reached for the handle, offering him a polite smile. "Like I said, I'm not interested. I've got a son and I have no intention of uprooting him."

Disappointment stabbed through him, surprising in its strength. He'd also heard about her son, so her refusal wasn't totally unexpected. What was unexpected was hearing himself offer, "I've got some employees that freelance for me. Work special jobs during their vacations. If you ever want to consider that, give me a call." He handed her a card, quoting the range of pay.

Her eyes widened, her first real reaction since they'd started the conversation. "A month?"

"A week. Of course, it depends on the job."

Looking bemused, she accepted the card and slipped it into the pocket of her jacket. "The bodyguard business must be lucrative."

"I prefer personal protection specialists, and yeah." He lifted a shoulder. "It's a dangerous world."

"Tell me about it." She opened the car door, got in. "Goodbye, McCabe."

He stepped away, watching her back out of the space. Leave the lot. And wondered why he was feeling so disappointed that a woman he barely knew was driving out of his life.

She might have made it in time to pick up Alex, Ava thought darkly, as she reparked her car in the half-empty police headquarters lot thirty minutes later. Probably would have, given that he always seemed to be the last one out of the locker room. But the terse phone call she'd received when she'd been halfway to the East High School gym had ended hopes of getting home any time soon.

Her mood grim, she jogged up the steps to the building and flashed her ID at the officer manning the front desk. She strode by with barely a pause in her step, heading toward the stairs leading to the administrative offices. Chief Sanders hadn't been particularly forthcoming on the phone. But it wasn't like she could turn down his "request" that she head back in for yet another meeting.

Questions tumbled through her mind like circus acrobats. Had a question arisen regarding Cabrerra's death? It had been a clean shoot, but she'd seen more than one SWAT sniper get caught up in bureaucratic bullshit after a public outcry.

She took the steps to the second floor two at a time. It was much too early for Sanders to be taking flak for the incident response. The nightly news had just aired. And the mayor, never her favorite person, wouldn't have a reaction until the results of his daily polls were weighed.

Since it was impossible to guess the agenda for the meeting, Ava tried to shove her questions aside. But that didn't dissipate the knot of nerves tightening in her stomach.

Knocking on the closed door of Sanders's office, she awaited the chief's growled invitation before entering. Immediately her gaze went to the strangers seated across the desk from the chief. She made them out as feds immediately. Their dark suits and arrogant expressions were more telling than badges.

"Detective Carter." Chief Sanders waved her toward a chair. Ava sat in one a couple feet from the strangers. She felt the two men's gazes on her, bold and appraising, so she returned their stares unflinchingly. With a few notable exceptions, she held feds in as low esteem as she did politicians, for much the same reasons.

"DHS Agents Samuelson and Paulus," Sanders continued, with what passed for an introduction. The men gave her slight nods, and Ava struggled to hide her jolt of shock. What would Homeland Security want with her? Because it was at their request that Sanders had ordered her back. That much was clear.

"I'm sure you're anxious to get home, Detective Carter," started Samuelson. He was a tall, spare man, with slicked-back thinning dark hair and a tan that didn't quite hide the old acne scars on his face. "I'll get right to the point. I understand from Chief Sanders that you've met Cael McCabe, the owner of Global Securities."

"Yes."

The agent seemed to be waiting for her to go on, but when she didn't, he pressed, "The two of you were seen together in the parking lot afterward."

"Yes." Seen by whom? Who had been the person of interest? McCabe or her?

A note of impatience crept into Samuelson's tone. "Did the two of you have a conversation?"

"Yes." She saw Sanders hide a smile at her less than enlightening responses. But she was damned if she was going to feed the feds any information before they extended her the same courtesy.

"We'd like to know what you discussed." It was the first time Agent Paulus had spoken, and Ava shifted her attention to him. He was a good foot shorter than Samuelson, stocky, with coarse gingery hair and nearly invisible eyebrows.

"Why?"

"Because we asked, Ms. Carter." Samuelson's omission of her title didn't escape her. Neither did his biting tone. She was familiar with the intimidation tactics feds could use to leverage information. She glanced again at Sanders and he gave her a small nod.

She leaned back in her chair, feigning nonchalance. "He offered me a job." The two agents exchanged a look. Clearly she'd startled them. But even more surprising was the suppressed excitement she sensed her words elicited from them.

"With Global Securities?" Samuelson barely waited for her nod before pressing, "And what was your answer?"

"I told him I wasn't interested." Her interest was piqued now, however.

"We'd like you to reconsider your answer to McCabe's job offer," Samuelson said. Though couched as a suggestion, it sounded more like a command. "There's a matter of national security you could assist with by doing so."

"Why would I do that?" She didn't understand Chief

Sanders's silence, but she was tiring of the subterfuge. And her diplomacy skills tended to thin when she was tired.

"Patriotism?" offered Paulus. "Duty to your country? Commitment to national freedom?"

Anger coursed through her, a hot rush of feeling. Although she knew she was being manipulated, she was helpless to stem her response. "I'm recently recovered·from taking a bullet because of my line of work. Just got back on the job two weeks ago. Tread carefully, gentlemen. You might not want to question my sense of duty."

"She's right." As if Sanders could remain quiet no longer, he came forward in his chair, aimed a steely look at the agents. "Detective Carter is a valued member of our force, and of our incident response unit. Time to fish or cut bait, gentlemen. If you want interagency cooperation, you have to be open about the mission you're asking Detective Carter's help on."

"Of course." Samuelson smoothed his muted striped tie, his manner stiff. "We were getting to that. Our agency has an interest in Antonio de la Reyes's new government and of the political climate in San Baltes. McCabe is providing security for de la Reyes, and anyone on his team would have access to certain… intelligence…that would help us with our threat assessment of the newly formed government there. With your heroics today, we thought you'd be in the perfect position to impress McCabe. Petition him for a position on his team." He gave her a small smile devoid of sincerity. "Obviously you already accomplished that feat. He was impressed enough to offer you a job, which would make your task even more plausible."

It was amazing, Ava thought cynically, what passed for open communication with these guys. Or maybe they really underestimated her intelligence enough that they thought she'd buy their story unquestioningly. "Why do you need me? Why not approach McCabe directly for the information?" She read her answer from the pained expressions on the agents' faces.

"Mr. McCabe was disinterested in cooperating."

Ava's lips quirked. She could imagine McCabe's response had been somewhat less polite than Samuelson indicated. Her estimation of the security consultant kicked up a notch.

"Well, I'm confused." She gave the agents an easy shrug. "The situation you're outlining sounds like a matter for the CIA, not DHS. Your involvement means there's a terrorism component to your concern. I must have missed it when you mentioned that part."

"This is extremely sensitive." Agent Paulus cast a look at the other agent as he spoke. "Whatever your response, I hope we can count on your discretion." He waited expectantly, but when Ava said nothing, he went on. "Alberto Martinez, the former leader of San Baltes, was a corrupt dictator. We have reason to believe money from his government was supporting terrorist attacks throughout South America. Naturally we're eager for the opportunity to explore the degree to which that network still exists. Your placement on McCabe's team gives us such an opportunity."

"I'm sorry." Her voice was insincere. "As I told Mr. McCabe, I have a job here. A teenage son to care for. I'm not free to take the job even if I wanted to."

"Captain Sanders assures us that your job would be waiting for you during your absence, as would your spot on SWAT. And your ex-husband could care for your son while you're gone, couldn't he?"

Everything in Ava stilled. Her glance flicked to the chief and back to Samuelson. It was impossible to be sure whether they'd gotten the personal details of her life from Sanders or from their own digging, but she'd bet on the latter. DHS wasn't known for their regard for individuals' privacy.

The only question remaining was how deep they'd dug.

"The answer's still no." Inwardly seething, Ava made sure her emotions didn't show in her expression. A sense of duty had formed her desire to enter the police force, but this…they were asking her to deceive McCabe, if in fact she could convince him to put her on de la Reyes's detail. To act as a spy while she was in San Baltes.

She'd worked plenty of undercover cases, but there was nothing compelling about the agents' request. They could cite national security all they wanted, but they'd failed to convince her of the urgency of this particular task. And even she was surprised at the level of distaste she felt for it.

"So that's it, gentlemen." Sanders rose, indicating the meeting was at an end. Ava couldn't tell if he approved of her response or not. "I said I'd release Detective Carter if she agreed, but you have her answer. I'm afraid I have another meeting in a few minutes."

They all rose, and the tall agent reached into his pocket to withdraw a card. He handed it to her. "In case you reconsider."

When Ava went to take it, the man didn't release the card immediately. Her gaze met his.

"Think it over, Ms. Carter." His voice was pitched low enough to reach only her ears. "I happen to believe a single act of patriotism can erase years of disloyalty. Years that might prove embarrassing should they be made public."

The freshly healed scar on her shoulder throbbed at his thinly veiled warning. He finally released the card and she slipped it into her suit pocket. Turning without a word, she headed for the door, wondering frantically just how thorough their investigation of her had been.

Because she didn't think she was imagining the threat in Samuelson's parting words.

Chapter 2

Once back in her car, Ava checked her cell phone and found a text message from Alex assuring her he'd find another ride home. She slipped the key in the ignition, but then sat still for a few moments, her fingers clenching and unclenching on the steering wheel.

It was ridiculous to let Samuelson rattle her. She was accustomed to the strong-arm tactics feds used to get what they wanted, but surely his was an empty threat. Her occupation was a daily testament to her patriotism. She didn't have to fly to another country to prove it. Just as she didn't have to constantly strive to negate her radical upbringing. How many times had her ex-husband reminded her of that?

Apparently, not often enough.

Perhaps she'd misinterpreted his words. Ava had the thought, tried to believe it. The assignment the man had described didn't seem all that vital to national security. So he'd left something out, hardly surprising when dealing with feds.

Which made it impossible to decide whether he'd been bluffing about making trouble for her.

She headed out of the lot and turned on the busy Belleview Boulevard. They lived on the outskirts of the city, a fact her son had grown to hate as his social relationships had become the center of his life. But at the time she and Danny had bought the property, it was quite a bit cheaper to live farther out. That was before trendy developments had started popping up all over in what had previously been a spacious, peaceful area.

Things changed. Ava slowed as she came up on a blue-haired woman who could barely see over the top of the steering wheel. Her neighborhood wasn't the only evidence of that. Less than five years after they'd bought the house, she and Danny had separated. They'd been divorced for nearly three years.

Turning at her corner, she immediately recognized the blue Toyota parked at the curb in front of her house. Her stomach plummeted. It had been a long, stressful day. She and her ex-husband had an amiable relationship, but she wasn't in the mood to deal with him tonight. All she wanted was a hot meal and a cold beer. Maybe sitting down with Alex to catch the Lakers game on ESPN.

All of which would have to wait until Danny was gone.

Pulling to a stop under the carport, she got out of the vehicle, leaving her gear locked in the trunk. Normally she'd put her rifle in the gun safe, but that would mean carrying it into the house and Danny had never hidden his disapproval about her participation on Alpha Squad. It had been one of the things that had driven them apart.

Pushing open the front door, she saw her ex-husband and Alex sitting on the couch talking animatedly. If their sudden silence at her appearance wasn't a tip-off that they were up to something, their guilty expressions would have been.

Ava closed the door behind her and raised a quizzical brow. "So, what are you two hatching?"

"Nothing." Her son was a horrible liar. His eyes, as dark

as her own, were alight with excitement. His entire body practically quivered with it. "Dad called right after your text, and when I told him I needed a ride he said he'd pick me up."

"Uh-huh." She grabbed him playfully as she walked by the couch, dropping a kiss on his brown mop of hair before he could dodge away. "Did you also tell him we're going shopping tomorrow and you have to get all your homework done tonight?"

"Oh man." Alex slumped against the couch. "Can't you just go and bring some stuff home for me to look at?"

She cocked her head, pretended to consider it. "You mean bring home different sizes and fashions for you to try on and then take back whatever you don't want? Sort of like your own personal shopper?"

"Yeah."

"Nope." Ava dropped in a chair and fixed Alex with a steady look. "Go on and do your English while I talk to your dad. I'll order something for supper."

His excitement visibly dimmed, Alex got up and slouched out of the room, muttering, "Okay, but the next kid I see at the mall that calls you a MILF, I'm gonna punch him in the face."

"Violence is never the answer, Alex," Danny said reprovingly.

But Ava was less focused on her ex-husband's words than she was on her son's. "What is that? MILF? He's complained about that before." She swung her puzzled gaze to Danny's, but her ex looked just as mystified as she was. She'd have to remember to ask one of the other cops. Danny wasn't exactly up on teenage vernacular.

"Thanks for bringing him home."

Her ex-husband took off his rimless glasses and cleaned the lenses on his shirt, his fine white-blond hair falling in his eyes. "I wanted to come by and talk to you tonight anyway. It worked out."

"Must be big." She waited for him to put his glasses back on, blink at her owlishly. "I haven't seen Alex that excited since the baseball coach moved him up to play JV last year."

"Well." Danny gave her that boyish smile that once would have softened something inside her. "It is big. But how big depends on you."

For the second time in an hour Ava found herself wishing for a beer. "Danny. It's been a long day. Just spill it, okay?"

He fingered his white collar, a nervous habit he had. "I just told him about a mission trip I have planned. I booked some flights to Tanzania for this summer for myself and a few other church members. We're going to help build some schools. Train teachers. I'll be gone the entire summer."

"That's longer than usual." She reached for the lever to kick up the footrest on her recliner and smothered a purr of satisfaction when the chair responded. "Your church must have really done some major fund-raising for this trip."

His gaze skirted hers. "The church remains committed to our missionary work. But with the upcoming renovations to the building planned…well, money is tight. I funded it myself."

"You…" Ava gaped at him. "You don't have any money." The child support he sent her was modest. His salary as assistant pastor in a small church was less than what she made, and cops weren't exactly featured on *Lifestyles of the Rich and Famous*. "Where would you get…" Her stomach plummeted. "Oh, Danny. Tell me you didn't."

He folded his hands on his knees and leaned forward, his choirboy face earnest. "These people are among the poorest in the world, Ava. They live in mud huts. Some of the children walk ten miles a day to school. Try to put things in perspective. If some personal sacrifice means we can help hundreds of less fortunate…"

The last thing she needed right now was another lecture on *sacrifice*. She came upright and out of the chair in one smooth motion, her fists balled at her sides. "The sacrifice is hardly personal when it's your son paying the price. Did you tell Alex you financed this trip by selling the bonds you were saving for his college costs?"

His chin squared. He'd never once raised his voice in all the years she'd known him, but she recognized that expression. It meant he wouldn't budge from his position. "You still have your savings for him, right? And he doesn't have to go to MIT. There's a perfectly adequate college right here in Metro City."

Ava closed her eyes, gritting her teeth against the hot words that trembled on her tongue. "He's talked of nothing else for three years. He got a two thousand on the SAT as a freshman, Danny. He's not going to the local college." Her son's proficiency in academics, especially in math and science, had been noticed early in elementary school. She'd been saving what she could for his future since then. They both had. At least until now.

"MIT gives need-based scholarships anyway. And if he has to borrow some money, he'll appreciate his education more." Danny's voice turned indulgent. "The Lord will provide, Ava. You just have to believe."

She stared at him, her breathing strangled. Which of them had changed more since they'd first met at seventeen and twenty? No real puzzle there. Danny was still the dreamy-eyed idealist, with the biggest heart she'd ever met. So big sometimes that it blinded him to the needs of his own family. While she…after eleven years on the force, she'd learned that all people weren't inherently good. That evil was more than a concept. And if you didn't take care of your own, no one else would.

Turning her back on him, she fought to keep her voice steady. "You need to go."

"Ava—"

"Now." She could feel the temper heating her from the inside out. The tightness in her chest heralded an impending explosion. Alex didn't need to hear his parents arguing. He'd heard plenty of that before they'd split.

There was nothing to argue about at any rate. The bonds were gone. And nothing she could say would convince Danny he'd violated a trust by using them.

A thought struck her there, comprehension piercing anger. She whirled to see Danny halfway through the door. "Wait." He halted. "That's not what had Alex so excited. What'd you tell him?"

His sheepish look was its own answer. "I meant to run it by you first. Really. But we got to talking, and seeing how interested he was, it just came out. But I warned him that you were going to have the final say, Ava. I swear I did."

"No."

"It would be a wonderful experience for him." Her ex let go of the doorknob and moved closer to her. "He'll learn compassion for others...."

"My son doesn't need to travel ten thousand miles to learn compassion." Her voice shook with the effort it took to keep it steady. Odd how she could face down an armed robber. Take out a target at a thousand yards. But this...this had panic sprinting down her spine. Ice bumping through her veins. "And if you think I'm sending a fifteen-year-old boy halfway around the world with you this summer, you are seriously deranged."

"Pizza delivery."

Ava stood in her son's open doorway and waved the pizza box in front of her. Alex turned around in his desk chair and grinned in delight. "Meat lover's with mushrooms and green olives?"

"Yes, O Gluttonous One." When she entered his room, her son's eyes widened. "I get to eat in my room?" The practice had been banned after Ava had discovered why the house had such an ant infestation. Alex tended to forget the leftovers he shoved under his bed, but the ants never did.

"It's a onetime offer, and mealtime rules apply. Put a shirt on." He must have showered, because his hair was damp and he was clad only in baggy basketball shorts. He got up and pulled a T-shirt over his head, and she was struck anew by the definition in his back and shoulders. He already stood eye-to-eye with her at five nine. He'd surpass her by his next birthday. Girls had been calling the house for three years, but in the last twelve months or so Alex had been doing some calling of his own. Sometimes the years seemed to meld into nanoseconds. Another few blinks and he'd be off to college and she'd be alone for the first time in her life.

Shrugging off the bolt of emotion that twisted at the thought, she sat on his bed, cross-legged, with the box on her lap. She handed him a plate as he reached for the first slice of pizza, knowing he wasn't one to bother with such niceties on his own.

"This looks great. What are you going to eat?"

"Funny." But Ava withdrew two pieces just in case. Alex could work his way through the rest without a pause. His metabolism should rank as one of the Seven Wonders of the World.

They ate for a few minutes in companionable silence. After breaking all speed limits to wolf down three slices, he finally slowed enough to say, "Guess you're pretty pissed that Dad talked to me about going to Africa, huh?"

At her sharp glance he rolled his eyes and amended, "I mean 'mad.'"

She put her half-eaten slice down and reached for a napkin. "It's a big decision, Alex. And it's one we should have talked over before he mentioned it to you. So yeah, I'm not crazy about the idea."

"But you'll think about it, right? I mean, how cool would that be? I've never even been out of the country before."

"You've been to Mexico."

He waved off her correction. "Okay, I haven't been off the continent. When would I ever get a chance like this again?"

She wiped her fingers carefully, trying to hide her dismay. "It wouldn't be a pleasure trip. You'd be working. Living without indoor plumbing and electricity. No TV. No video games."

"I know that." He took another slice out of the box. "But I'd be doing some good, right? And think how that would look on my college application. You're always saying I need to list community service."

"I was thinking more like mentoring middle schoolers. Teaching Sunday school. And what about baseball?"

"Dad said I could fly out after the regular season is done. It's not like we're going to State this year. Not with Severin as the pitcher. Did you know his fastball is only clocked at sixty miles an hour?"

She had to smile at the disgusted expression on his face.

"So that would give me a good month there before I have to come back and get ready for school."

The bite Ava had just taken turned to ash in her mouth. She swallowed with effort. "What about our camping trip?" Each year she saved the majority of her vacation and they went to the mountains. Or the desert. Or the Southwest. They spent weeks poring over maps, planning their route and which campsites to stop at. Where to hike or kayak. They'd been talking about white-water rafting on the Snake River on their travels this summer.

Alex shrugged. "We camp every year. It's no big deal." Then he looked up, his face stricken. "I mean, we can go again next summer, right?"

He had a heart as soft as Danny's. Ava knew if she didn't reassure him, he'd beat himself up for hurting her feelings. "Right. But I still have to think about it."

"Okay." He reached for another slice, satisfied for the time being with her answer. But when he changed the topic to complain about a teacher who just happened to teach his least favorite subject—English—Ava's attention was only half on the conversation.

Her mind was reeling. First there'd been the unsettling meeting with DHS, then the double punch of the twin parental concerns she'd been handed tonight.

Experiencing a sinking certainty, Ava was beginning to believe that the solution to all three situations might be entwined.

"So, do you?"

Her attention jerked back to her son, who was regarding her impatiently. "Do I what?"

"Have some sort of genealogy information for me to use for this lame English paper."

Ava searched through the fragments of the last few moments of conversation that had registered, came up empty. "Why do you need that?"

Alex rolled his eyes. "Mo-om. I just told you about that family tree assignment Fulton gave us in English. I need something to put in the paper I have to write. Five pages. Five. Whole. Pages."

Ordinarily she would have commiserated with her son's dismay. She wasn't much of a writer herself. But for the second time that day she was reminded of her past, and it wasn't a recollection she cared for.

"I'm sorry, my family wasn't much for writing stuff like that down." That, at least, was the truth. She knew her grandparents' names but that was about it.

"No living relative you can get information from?"

She thought of her father then, the accompanying twist of pain familiar. "No." The lie didn't weigh heavily on her. She'd spent the first two years of Alex's life desperately trying to get her father to acknowledge her existence, and that of his grandson.

And then the next dozen years ignoring his.

"Great." Alex wadded up his napkin and slouched in his chair. "Now Fulton will make me take the information you do have and do a genealogy search on the Internet. Jonnie Winters had to do that last semester and it took him days. I was hoping just to write the report with what we already had."

Tiny shards of ice formed in Ava's blood. All sorts of information was available on the Internet. But one thing would not be found there: any trace of her father's death.

She considered for a moment having to explain to her son

why she'd lied to him all these years about their lack of relatives. Thought of how she'd tell him who and what his grandfather was. Who Ava used to be.

Her throat suddenly dry, she looked at Alex, who was regarding her expectantly. "How about you use your dad's genealogy for the paper? Grandpa Carter has notebooks full of their family history."

Hope glimmered in her son's eyes. "You think I could? It's not exactly my family since dad adopted me."

"Well, you share the same last name, so Mr. Fulton won't know that, will he?"

"Sweet," he said with satisfaction. "I thought of that earlier, but I thought…you know…maybe you'd think it was dishonest or something."

Ava caught Alex's eyes on her and it was all she could do not to squirm. Her hypocrisy weighted heavily on her. She'd endlessly preached truthfulness to her son while she'd spent his whole life lying to him about her family.

She smiled weakly, guilt slashing at her. There was little a parent wouldn't do to protect her child. But sometimes she wondered whom she was really protecting. Because in that moment she realized exactly how far she'd go to keep her past hidden, for both their sakes.

Cael stepped out of the shower and carelessly swiped a towel down his body as he reached for his ringing cell. It was after eleven, West Coast time. But he had operatives across the nation and in several countries with various time zones. And in accordance with Murphy's Law, it seemed like at least half of them had called with some sort of problem today.

He looked at the screen, didn't recognize the number. "Global Security." As he answered the call he fastened the towel around his waist, raking his fingers through his hair. Maybe he could manage a haircut before leaving the States again.

"McCabe."

That low smoky tone was immediately recognizable. So was the heat it elicited low in his belly. "Ava Carter."

There was a hesitation. Then, "I just noticed the time. I didn't realize it was so late."

"Not a problem. All hell's been breaking loose this evening and I haven't even thought about sleep yet." He headed out to the sitting area of his suite, perched on the arm of the couch, intrigued and wary. When they'd parted this afternoon he'd never expected to see her again. And he still had trouble understanding the source of the regret that thought had elicited.

But then later, when Benton had reported following Samuelson to police headquarters, where Carter had reappeared, too, his interest in her had taken on a whole different facet.

She didn't beat around the bush. "I've been thinking of your offer this afternoon. About short-term employment. Were you serious?"

His stomach twisted, a quick vicious lurch. It took more effort than it should have to respond evenly. "Yeah. How much time do you have available?"

"I have several weeks' leave accumulated."

"Then you could take some now, right?" With the words he baited the trap, prayed she wouldn't walk in. Heard it snap closed when she did.

"I could probably get approval for immediate leave."

"If you're serious about this I'd like to meet with you as soon as possible." Needed to, to find out what had caused her sudden about-face.

But he was very much afraid he already knew.

"All right. My shift tomorrow gets done at—"

"Tomorrow I'm flying to L.A. It'll have to be tonight." He crossed to the desk, found a pad and pen. "Give me directions to your place. I'll be there in thirty minutes." The reluctance in her voice as she recited the directions did nothing to dispel the determination spiking in his gut. As he disconnected the phone he clenched the instrument tightly in his hand, to avoid hurling it across the room. He didn't want to believe that DHS had drawn her into this. It would be a stretch, even for Samuelson.

But the possibility had to be explored. He crossed to his suitcase, pulled out some clothes. Dropping the towel, he began to dress swiftly. The fact that he was reluctant to credit the suspicions forming in his mind meant Ava Carter had already gotten under his skin.

Which made her dangerous in more ways than one.

The expression on Ava's face was wary as she pulled open the door before Cael had a chance to knock. Stepping aside to let him in, she said, "You move fast."

"I have to." Stepping inside, he shot a quick look around the place as she closed the door behind him. "I've got a killer schedule and we're spread a little thinner than I'd like."

He followed her to the leather couch and sat down, while she seated herself in the recliner facing him. On the way over he'd convinced himself that his earlier reaction to her was a combination of adrenaline and respect. That shot of hers today had been an impressive depiction of her talent.

But looking at her now, he realized he'd been kidding himself. Adrenaline had long faded, and it wasn't exactly respect that had him noticing her long, slim legs. Or the very female curves beneath the T-shirt she wore.

"So being shorthanded is the reason you wanted me to take vacation immediately?"

Her question yanked his attention back to business, where it would need to stay. If she was linked to Samuelson he'd have to tread carefully.

"Partially. But I've accepted an extension to my contract with de la Reyes. And your skills would come in useful during the course of that case."

Cael leaned back and propped one foot over the opposite knee, settling deeper into the couch. "De la Reyes needs personal protection more than ever. There's a rebel faction in his country working for a man who wants him out of power. With Cabrerra's betrayal, he can't afford to trust anyone. If his security detail has been infiltrated, why not his government? His household help? He needs outsiders to spearhead a safety regimen for him, until he can weed out those whose loyalty can be bought."

"And what happens to those people?"

He recognized the concern in her question. "Don't worry. Whatever you think of de la Reyes's politics, he came to power through a democratic election. He's lobbying our government for increased aid. He's hardly going to jeopardize that with civil rights violations. Those disloyal to him would be expelled from the country or jailed, but he wouldn't order them killed. He says he's committed to having his country recognized by the U.N. after decades of dictator rule. I believe him."

Ava looked less certain. "And the immediacy you spoke of earlier?"

"I need to accompany de la Reyes to L.A., which will be his last stop in the States. In two days we fly back to San Baltes. It'll take ten operatives to provide full security for him there once he resumes his full schedule. I can't have them all in place for at least a week."

"So I'd be providing protection until you can put a team together."

"*We'd* be providing protection," Cael corrected. "At least until the full detail is positioned. Are you as skilled with a handgun as you are with a rifle?"

She regarded him coolly. "Yes."

"Good. You'll be provided with both. I can expedite a passport if you don't have one."

"I do."

Giving a satisfied nod, he said, "So it's just a matter of getting the time off on short notice."

She raised her brows. "There's a matter of me agreeing first."

He didn't smile but something inside him lightened. Dead

tired, he shouldn't find it so damn stimulating to spar with her. Especially given what she might be hiding from him. "Ava, if you weren't interested you wouldn't have contacted me. Something changed between the time I spoke to you this afternoon and when you called earlier. Something that made you overlook your earlier objections."

She'd gone still, but not a flicker of expression crossed her face. "I'm not a cop, but I do have some deductive powers. That's how I keep my clients alive." He sat, barely breathing, waiting for her reply. Wanting desperately for her to prove those persistent little doubts swirling inside him wrong.

For a moment he thought she wouldn't answer. Was prepared to probe further. But then she said, her gaze skirting his, "After a visit from my ex-husband this afternoon I find myself in need of money." Her eyes came back to fix on his then, held steady. "If I decide to do this, regardless of my reasons, I'll put everything I've got into the assignment. I won't take it if I don't believe I can be of help to you."

He almost lost his train of thought for a moment, under her liquid chocolate gaze, before his resolve hardened. Nodding, he got to his feet, headed toward the door. "You check on that vacation time in the morning. I'll need your answer in twenty-four hours."

Closing the door behind him, he jogged down the steps toward his car. He could ill-afford to turn down her help if she did sign on. He hadn't been lying about needing her on de la Reyes's protection team.

But had *she* been lying to *him*?

He opened the door of the dark rental sedan, slid inside. Her story about a sudden need for money was plausible. It was also completely impossible to check out. Starting the ignition, he pulled away from the curb. Useless to wonder if it was a story cooked up between her and Samuelson. Or to speculate what her motivation would be for agreeing to join forces with the man.

He wanted—needed—to take her word at face value. But

Cael McCabe believed in being prepared. As much as he believed in revenge.

He glanced in his rearview mirror before switching lanes. If Ava Carter turned out to be working with Samuelson, he'd have no compunction about using her to destroy the man. And if that destroyed her in the process, well...

She would have gotten exactly what she deserved.

Chapter 3

Two days later Ava was jogging across the tarmac at LAX to the private jet waiting for her. A man she remembered from Cael's security detail at the civic center stood at the base of the steps leading into the plane. She flipped through her mental Rolodex. Bailey. Balsem. Benton. That was it. He'd been flanking de la Reyes's other side when Cabrerra fired at the man, hitting the officer instead. He was around her age, with wavy brown hair and a friendly puppy dog face that belied the seriousness of his occupation.

When she would have hurried up the steps by him, he reached for her bag. "I'll take care of this."

"I can handle it."

"Sorry." He didn't relinquish his grip on the suitcase. "Boss's orders."

Ava released the bag, hoping her uneasiness didn't show. She'd refused most of the high-tech tools Samuelson had tried to press on her, but she had accepted the minicamera hidden inside what looked like a normal pen. All parts were plastic or ceramic to pass undetected through security.

Heading into the jet, she reassured herself it was unlikely the item would raise any concerns. She was a cop, and she wouldn't have found the tiny camera if it hadn't been shown to her. It certainly looked harmless enough, clipped to a slim notepad in a zippered side compartment.

She paused before heading down the aisle. The surroundings were considerably more opulent than any she'd flown in before. There were six rows with two wide, comfortable-looking leather seats on either side of the aisle. Through an open door in the back she noted another compartment complete with wet bar and couches.

McCabe was seated midway back next to de la Reyes, and the two discontinued their conversation when she made an appearance. The president spoke first.

"Detective Carter." His face was wreathed in smiles. "It is a pleasure to see you again. Forgive me for not rising. My seat belt is fastened in preparation for departure."

Cael lifted a brow at her. "You cut it close," he noted.

Her nerves jittered. Considering the fact that she'd had to completely rearrange both her personal and private life in less than forty-eight hours, it was a miracle she'd made it on time.

And given her continued ambivalence about this task, it would have been a relief if the jet had taken off without her.

As the men resumed their conversation she took a free seat near the back behind an operative of Cael's she remembered from before. Sibbits, she thought his name was. He was exceedingly thin, as if all excess flesh had been carved away. His receding hairline was graying, and cropped short. The rest of the plane's occupants were part of de la Reyes's entourage.

Benton boarded the plane, minus her bag, and took a seat up front. It didn't take a rocket scientist to know that her luggage had been thoroughly searched before it had been stowed. The precaution only served to remind her of the precariousness of her situation. Until de la Reyes ascertained the level of infiltration, no one in his government was above suspicion.

And if Ava let her guard down in the slightest, a very different sort of suspicion would fall on her.

The jet's engines revved. Moments later it began rolling along the runway. She'd never been a nervous flier, but the anxiety from her situation had her remaining seated upright, muscles tight with tension. So it must have been sheer exhaustion that had her asleep before they'd been in the air a half hour.

Awareness prickled beneath her subconscious. In the dim recesses of her mind, an alarm shrilled. Ava struggled to surface from slumber, but it was like swimming against a powerful current. She couldn't manage to drag her eyes open.

She was floating in pale green seas, being tugged ashore by an unrelenting tide. The sensation might have been pleasant if she'd felt more in control. As it was, she fought against the inexorable force of nature, found herself betrayed by limbs that had turned weak and molten.

Opening her eyes, she was disoriented to see Cael's face close to hers, his gaze fixed and intense. It was with no little embarrassment that she realized his eyes were the exact shade of the sea she'd been lost in only moments ago. Sleep shredded defenses and dignity with equal ease. Exploited vulnerabilities usually kept guarded.

"We'll be landing in fifteen minutes."

Averting her gaze, she raised her seat forward. "You should have wakened me earlier."

"I figured you probably needed the sleep. It couldn't have been easy making all the arrangements you had to on such short notice."

The innocent words had remorse stabbing through her. She'd called him before she'd contacted DHS, half hoping he'd make the decision easy for her. If he hadn't invited her along on this particular mission, she would have been off the hook, having done her "duty."

But he hadn't made it easy for her. And neither had Samuelson, with his air of condescension, as if her eventual acquiescence had never been in question. She didn't know which made her feel worse, that she was deceiving a man who paid her salary for the duration of the job. Or that the money itself had played an undeniable part in her decision.

Turning back to McCabe, she said only, "What's in place so far?" Regardless of Samuelson's agenda for this trip, she was being paid to provide security protection, and that task would take precedence while she was in San Baltes.

His voice was pitched low. "I've got two men on the ground already. They'll have completed some preliminary work prior to our arrival. De la Reyes was originally scheduled to return to San Baltes tomorrow. His men, including the pilot, just found out this morning of the change of plans. I've tried to make sure none of them have had access to outside communication."

She asked shrewdly, "And the news of his early return has been leaked only to…?"

Cael gave her an approving look. "Rafael Gonzalez is de la Reyes's chief of Presidential Guard. It'd be like our Secret Service. Pedro Cabrerra was his most senior officer."

Ava's spine prickled as she grasped his meaning. "Even if Gonzalez shares Cabrerra's political leanings, he'd be crazy to try anything now. He has to realize his department will already be under suspicion."

"Which also makes it more urgent that he act. His entire branch is about to undergo intense scrutiny. If Gonzalez is affiliated with the rebels, he has one last chance to strike before his access to President de la Reyes becomes curtailed."

She nodded her understanding. "How do we know the rest of his security detail weren't in on Cabrerra's plan?"

Cael looked grim. "That's one of the questions my operatives are checking into. They're investigating all Cabrerra's associates, discreetly, of course. I have them meeting us at the airport to provide more security for the trip to the presidential palace."

"What will we have for weapons?"

"We'll have access to enough firepower to hold off a small rebel contingent." At her sharp glance, the corner of his mouth turned up. "Let's hope it's not needed. Our team will take over as the first security wave. The nationals will answer to us for now. You'll be in a rotation providing personal protection to de la Reyes at all times." His gaze raked her form. "I've got a vest for you. You'll wear it every minute you're on duty. And with the exception of the limited amount of time you'll spend sleeping, you'll always be on duty." He waited a moment before saying quietly, "Regrets?"

"I don't waste time on regrets." It was almost true. There was no way to make amends for her past. No reason why she should feel the need to. Most of the time she believed that. But Samuelson had unerringly pressed exactly the right button to have that old guilt rising to the surface again.

"Good to know."

There was something in his eyes, in his voice that had her glancing at him. Found him watching her, in much the same way he'd been when she'd first wakened. A slow heat suffused her body just recalling that moment. But she knew none of her inner embarrassment showed on her face. She'd learned long ago how to mask her emotions.

"You're completely still when you sleep." His voice had gone whisper soft. "Like a porcelain statue. Not even your expression changes. I imagine you're like that when you're in position for a shot."

There was something curiously intimate in knowing that he'd watched her while she slept. No one else had ever had the opportunity, with the exception of her ex. She'd never "slept" with Alex's birth father. Not in the literal sense.

She could feel heat crawling up her neck. Cael McCabe had a knack for catching her off guard, and that would have to change. She knew enough about him to realize he was a man to seize any vulnerability and turn it to his advantage.

She was already vulnerable enough. The deception she was engaged in made an undeniably dangerous situation even more explosive.

As the jet idled on the runway Ava donned her vest, then sat down to check the weapons she'd been assigned. Two men she didn't recognize had carried them aboard from one of the three black SUVs parked nearby. Both were beauties, the handgun a nine-millimeter Lugar semiautomatic and a Remington rifle and scope that could have been twins to her SWAT equipment. She strapped on her holster and clipped the pouch of extra ammunition around her waist. Looking around, she saw everyone else similarly equipping themselves, with the exception of de la Reyes, who was speaking on a cell phone. She had protective garb for him, too, before he exited the jet.

She waited patiently as McCabe spoke quietly to the newcomers. They must be the men he said he had on the ground already, gathering intelligence. Switching her attention to the dark waiting vehicles, she surmised McCabe's plan. The best way to arrange security would be to have the armored cars drive right up to the jet, load the bags and leave without ever entering the airport building. With a VIP like de la Reyes on board, she imagined, that wouldn't be difficult to arrange.

McCabe and the two strangers got up and headed toward the door. Cael turned back, caught her eye. "Be ready to move out in five minutes."

She nodded, rising to approach de la Reyes. He was speaking in rapid-fire Spanish, most of which she was able to follow. She was familiar enough with the language to converse with Hispanic victims on the job. She heard him tell whomever he was speaking to that he'd be arriving home tomorrow. So he was following Cael's orders, at least for now. And from his tone, she thought he was speaking to a woman. McCabe hadn't mentioned a wife, so maybe a girlfriend.

Glancing out the window, she saw McCabe walking close to the side of one of the SUVs, a long pole in his hand. Checking for bombs on the undercarriage of the vehicle, she noted with approval. He was leaving nothing to chance. The mirror on the other end of the pole would reveal anything hidden beneath. She had no doubt that the interior would be subjected to a similarly rigorous search.

Her spine prickled. His thoroughness was a chilling reminder that de la Reyes hadn't been delivered to safety once he'd reached his homeland. Just the opposite.

Once de la Reyes ended the conversation, Ava slid into the seat next to him. "You'll need to put this on before leaving the aircraft." She handed him his vest. "Just as a precaution."

The man eyed the garment for a moment before reaching for it. "Mr. McCabe leaves nothing to chance."

Ava helped him into the vest, expertly fastening it for him. "That quality of his will work in your favor. Your situation calls for caution."

His expression was rueful. "I am a man of action. But we must take care first that I live to take that action, true?"

"That's right."

De la Reyes peered out the window. "How much longer will it be? I have much to do now that I am back."

"This is all just routine, but as I said, McCabe is a stickler for precautions."

"So I see," he murmured, his gaze returning to the window. "He is, as we say in my country, *un hombre de la guerra*. A man of war, is he not?"

His words jolted her, they so closely resembled her own impression in the briefing just a few short days ago. A warrior. Ready for battle at a moment's notice.

For the first time she wondered about McCabe's background. Not his security business, which she'd thoroughly checked out before calling him. But whatever had prepared him for establishing the business. Military, certainly. Special forces, most likely. It would explain that tough edge he maintained that the most civilized of garments or surroundings couldn't quite mask.

One of the vehicles pulled up to the aircraft steps. Ava led de la Reyes to the doorway. She and Benton flanked the man as they hurried him to the waiting SUV.

McCabe was behind the wheel, Sibbits next to him. Ava had de la Reyes get in the middle with Benton, while she positioned herself in the third seat next to a large leather duffel bag. The president's men split up into the remaining vehicles. One of McCabe's operatives rode in each of them. When one SUV pulled out, they followed, and the third brought up the rear.

Cael turned around. He'd donned a pair of mirrored sunglasses. "The gear's on the seat next to you."

Ava leaned over to unzip the bag. Spreading it open, she blinked.

It was packed to launch a small war.

There were several grenades, extra weapons and what looked like a portable rocket launcher. There were rifle scopes, binoculars, night-vision goggles and extra ammunition. Ava looked up, caught McCabe's eyes on her in the rearview mirror. He'd prepared himself for anything.

She withdrew a pair of German-made high-powered binoculars and trained them out the back window. Cordoba was the capital city of San Baltes, surrounded by mountains on three sides and the Pacific Ocean on the other. The natural beauty of the surroundings was in stark contrast to the Third World squalor they traveled through on the highway heading toward the center of the city.

"I'm a big fan of one of your country's singers. Mirabel Estaban. Have you ever met her?" Benton asked de la Reyes.

"Ah, Senorita Estaban. She is very talented, yes? She sang at my inauguration celebration. Her music is very popular here."

"I saw her on YouTube. On the Internet? She was wearing this dress cut down to…" Ava glanced up in time to see Sibbits turn in his seat, directing a look at Benton, who spread his hands innocently. "What? It showed her talents, is all I'm saying. Plus she can really sing."

De la Reyes gave a deep-throated laugh. "You are a man to appreciate a gorgeous woman. I can assure you, my country has many such beauties. Perhaps you will have the opportunity to meet some of them in your stay here."

Ava returned to her vigil, tuning out the conversation. There were three lanes of traffic traveling in either direction, separated by a median filled with mud, weeds and debris. Their American-made SUVs stood out among the economy-sized vehicles zipping by them.

Something caught her eye and she stilled, peering hard through the binoculars. The late-model Jeep coming up fast in the next lane behind them looked familiar.

"Alert car 3, vehicle to their back and left. We saw that red Jeep when we left the airport. Again when we took the last exit. Three occupants. No, wait. Four."

A radio crackled, and then she heard Sibbit's voice. "Vehicle three, ready defensive tactics. Red Jeep with multiple occupants. Left lane, coming fast."

The Jeep drew nearer and Ava felt a familiar spike of adrenaline. "Weapons sighted. At least two rifles."

Sibbits repeated the information to the third vehicle, while she heard McCabe speaking into his own radio, ordering the first SUV to drop back and exchange places with them. Benton was urging de la Reyes onto the floor, while he grabbed his weapon.

Ava lowered the high-powered glasses long enough to duck out from under the rifle strap, and readied the weapon. Sliding off the safety, she steadied the rifle, sighted, waiting for the command. The third vehicle swerved behind them into the path of the red Jeep, to force it to decrease its speed.

Except it didn't slow down. The Jeep slammed into the SUV, and there was a screech of metal on metal. Gunfire was exchanged between the two vehicles.

"Do you have a shot?"

Ava peered through the rifle's site, readjusted position to make up for the trajectory through two windows. "Yes."

"Take it."

The Jeep rammed the third SUV again, sending it spinning into the side rail. Ava saw the man in the Jeep's front passenger seat swing his rifle toward their vehicle as it raced toward them. Ignoring him for the moment, she concentrated on the driver, and squeezed the trigger once. Twice.

The Jeep's windshield shattered and the vehicle jerked to the right as the driver slumped over the wheel. The shooter's shot went wild. Ava saw the passenger in the front seat lower his weapon to wrench at the wheel as it veered into the far lane of traffic in front of an open-bed truck hauling a load of caged chickens.

"Vehicle one dropping back."

The bullet hole through their back window sent out a spiderweb of cracks, ruining her visual. She reengaged the safety and swung a leg over the seat to kick the window out with one booted foot. Their SUV picked up speed, lengthening the distance away from the Jeep. She saw the other SUV's occupants returning fire with the shooters in the Jeep before it careened into the median, flipping over on its top.

Ava could hear Cael snapping orders, Sibbits trying to raise vehicle three's occupants on the radio. De la Reyes was on the phone commanding a police helicopter to contain the scene. But then the Jeep burst into flames.

There would be very little for the police to investigate once they finally arrived.

* * *

"I owe you thanks once again, Senorita Carter."

Ava shifted uncomfortably, sliding a sidelong glance toward Cael. "It was a team effort, sir."

They stood in the sitting room of de la Reyes's opulent personal quarters on the third level of the presidential palace. Antonio stood at a wet bar tucked in a corner, pouring himself a glass of wine. For the first time since she'd met the man she could read weariness on his face.

"It was, yes." He gave her a small smile as he offered her a glass of wine. Because she could think of no polite way to refuse, Ava took it. "And I have already conveyed my gratitude to Senor McCabe."

"Have you compiled the list I asked for?" Cael accepted the wine Antonio held toward him.

"I have. It is there for you, on top of the desk." De la Reyes raised his own glass and drank deeply as he turned to face them. Lowering the glass, he added, "It includes every person in my government, along with their position. I do not like to suspect any of the names on it." He gave them a grim smile. "Only one of them learned the date of my arrival from me."

Cael crossed to the desk and picked up the paper, scanning it quickly before lifting his gaze to meet the other man's. "The men you had in the States with you…I collected their cell phones prior to them boarding. It would have been nearly impossible for them to communicate our plans prior to boarding the plane."

"So that means Rafael Gonzalez has betrayed me?" De la Reyes dropped heavily into an ornately carved chair that looked to be centuries old. "He has been with me since before I won the presidency. I would have trusted him with my life. I have done so, on countless occasions."

Lifting a shoulder, Cael said, "We have to take precautions. I'll want to interrogate him, of course. We've already got him placed under house arrest. He'll be detained until we can be certain."

Antonio's head jerked up, the hopeful expression on his face impossible to miss. "You think he could be innocent? How can that be?"

"The pilot had to file a flight plan. It could be someone in the airport. Hell, someone in the tower might have been paid to tip off your enemies whenever your flight plan was received."

"Then we still have no way to be certain who has been disloyal, or whom they alerted. I do not see that we are any further ahead then we were in Metro City."

Cael gave a feral smile. "Leave it to me. Our investigation is already under way. I'll need access to the bank accounts of every name on that paper you compiled for me, as soon as possible."

De la Reyes nodded. "You shall have it. I'll make the calls first thing in the morning."

"Then I'll have some answers for you in a matter of days."

Antonio raised his glass in a silent salute. "I will wish you luck, then, Mr. McCabe, since your success may mean my survival."

Sibbits drew duty outside de la Reyes's quarters that night, so the rest of the crew gathered in a conference room on the first floor of the palace. While Benton and Cael swept it for electronic bugs, Ava mentally calculated the last time she'd gotten a full night's sleep. Since the answer was too dismal to contemplate, she dismissed it. It didn't appear to be changing any time in the near future.

Finally, everyone settled into a chair around the table. She was reminded of the briefing that had taken place after the shooting…was it only two days ago? Two and a half?

Cael made introductions. "Mike Reynolds and Luis Perez have made some inroads since they got here two days ago. I'll let them bring you up to date."

Ava turned her attention to the two men he indicated, the ones who'd had the vehicles and weapons waiting for them at the airport.

Both were swarthy and dark complexioned, although Reynolds was taller and leaner than the stocky Perez. She knew instinctively that McCabe had chosen them for their ability to blend in with the San Baltes residents. If they were fluent in Spanish, they wouldn't raise suspicion mingling in the markets and cantinas ferreting out information.

Reynolds lost no time. "De la Reyes is highly unpopular with some factions." He stood, handing out thick files to each of them. "Especially by those who support the deposed dictator, Alberto Martinez. But we don't think Martinez is the threat. For one thing, he's been in exile in Brazil for three years. His supporters don't look good for the assassination attempt. We couldn't find any indication that they have the organization to move in once de la Reyes is out of the way."

He stopped, and Perez took over. "It's more likely that the attempt was financed by this man." He held up a picture. "Enrico Ramirez. He's the leader of a very powerful drug cartel that operated out of San Baltes for two decades, apparently with Martinez's knowledge and approval. Like most of the drug lords in the South American countries, he runs his drugs down the river systems in the jungle. De la Reyes has been cracking down on criminal elements in the country, and although he hasn't managed to catch Ramirez, his efforts have seriously curtailed the man's activities, and profits. He's had forensic accountants secretly going through the banks' records for months, hoping to find those Ramirez is funneling his money through."

Ava studied the man in the picture. Plump and avuncular, he looked more like a favorite uncle than a ruthless drug dealer.

"Ramirez went into hiding two years ago, but it's believed that he's financing the rebel contingent that has been causing such unrest in the country for the last eighteen months."

"He's using them to get rid of de la Reyes so he can go back to business as usual," Cael surmised aloud. "Does he want Martinez back in control?"

"We don't think so." Reynolds spoke for the two of them.

"Apparently Martinez got too greedy. It's more likely that Ramirez will just install a puppet president that will do his bidding while he gets his drug trade moving freely again."

"So if this attempt wasn't politically motivated," Ava said, "that means Cabrerra's betrayal was bought and paid for by Ramirez. That doesn't help us protect de la Reyes, but it might make it easier to determine if anyone else in his government is prepared to turn on him."

Cael nodded. "We follow the money. Did anything come up on the rest of de la Reyes's security contingent he brought with him to the States?"

Perez shook his head. "No. But that doesn't mean they're in the clear yet."

"Follow up on them, then. Also the pilot of the presidential jet." Cael gave them the man's name and Reynolds jotted it down. "Find out who was working the control tower today. Any one of them could have accessed the flight plan and alerted a third party."

Sibbits spoke up. "Did you get any information from the occupants in the Jeep today?"

McCabe shook his head grimly. "Ava took out the driver and Perez got the passenger in the front seat. The two in the back were trapped inside the vehicle. Identification of the bodies will be difficult."

Remembering the flames that had engulfed the Jeep, Ava felt a quick shudder. It would have been a grisly death. But she wasn't going to waste sympathy on the unknown assailants. Not when she knew their intent.

"De la Reyes will elicit the cooperation of the banks in the country. A little forensic accounting will tell us if anyone working in his government is sitting on some unexplained piles of cash. That will help us eliminate people quickly."

He slid a gaze around the table. "Sibbits, Carter and Benton will take turns protecting de la Reyes, in eight-hour shifts. You'll be backed up by his guard detail, but don't trust any of them until they've been cleared. When you're not on duty, you'll be at my side assisting in the investigation. De la Reyes will be changing his schedule of public appearances and conducting business out of the palace until further notice.

"Reynolds and Perez will follow up on the pilot and the airport tower personnel. Stay on top of the local police. We need IDs on the occupants in that Jeep."

"There's one more thing."

All eyes turned to Reynolds. "Perez and I have both heard talk about the rebels' jungle camp. I think if enough money changed hands, we might be able to get its location."

Cael thought for a moment. "How reliable is this information?"

The two operatives looked at each other. "We both heard the same rumors," Reynolds said. "The guy who claims he's been there…" The man lifted one shoulder. "I'd make sure he showed me sort of proof before I gave him any cash."

"How much?"

He named a price that seemed ridiculously low to Ava. But, she reminded herself, she was in a country with a per capita income of three thousand American dollars a year. Where allegiance could be bought if pockets were deep enough.

And where lives could be snuffed out for the price of a week's groceries.

"If you can verify the location and the function of the camp, go for it. These places tend to be portable, though. Find out if he knows other sites they've maintained." Seemingly finished, Cael looked at each of them in turn. "I don't have to remind you to be careful. Our mission is to keep de la Reyes alive long enough to find out who he can trust. After that he can better protect himself. But if we can point him in Ramirez's direction before we leave…" He gave a ruthless smile. "That will be gravy. Maybe he'll be able to clean up the country for good."

* * *

Cael had insisted on accompanying Ava to her room. And after her initial protest—one that had done very little good— she gave in. She still hadn't gotten her bearings. The place looked more like an estate than a palace, but the interior was certainly lavish enough to qualify as palatial.

"We're on the second floor, in the back of the building," he told her. She heard weariness in his voice, although there were no visible signs of it. His shoulders were still straight, his gaze alert as he assessed their surroundings. "Our quarters are directly above the kitchen area."

"Where are we located from the president's quarters?"

"He has the entire floor above us. Not ideal, but at least we don't have to fear infiltration through the windows. If someone wants to get to him at night, they'd have to get through several layers of security."

"Security that we can't trust," she reminded him. The precariousness of their situation was disquieting. If Cabrerra had been acting alone, de la Reyes was as safe in his palace as he could be anywhere. But if his superior was involved… "If Gonzalez turns out to be dirty, the entire presidential guard is suspect." And if the drug dealer Ramirez had gotten to two individuals so close to the San Baltes president, it was a wonder de la Reyes had survived this long.

She made a mental note to mention the drug dealer's name to Samuelson when she returned. If Ramirez was intent in keeping the region unstable, he might not be above financing terrorists acts toward that end. Not for the first time, she wondered how much the DHS agent already knew. He hadn't told her all the details in his possession. She could figure that much.

"We assume nothing," Cael agreed. He stopped before a door and reached to open it for her. "But I thought the attempt today by the men in the Jeep was encouraging."

Ignoring the opulent bedroom before her, she stared hard

at him. "Encouraging. The way an earthquake is encouraging? A train wreck?"

He didn't smile, but his face lightened a fraction. Leaning a shoulder against the doorjamb, he folded his arms. "Poor choice of words, maybe. But the fact that another attempt was made before de la Reyes made it to the palace makes me think this place isn't seen as vulnerable. Either Ramirez doesn't have anyone else with easy access to de la Reyes, or the president's security makes an attempt here seem high risk. Either would be good news for us. Even if Gonzalez is involved, perhaps Cabrerra was his only accomplice."

Although she didn't share his optimism, she didn't contradict him. "I'm assuming you've taken precautions with the guard personnel since we haven't cleared any of them yet."

He stifled a yawn. The gesture made him seem a bit more human. Up until now, she'd been half convinced the man was part machine. "Gonzalez is bound and confined to quarters. One of us will have to be posted outside until the evidence condemns or clears him. We've got nationals at every entrance of the palace, stationed three deep every twelve feet. If someone got past the outer perimeter of security, he'd have to get past a slug of armed guards. The chances are minimal that every one of the guards stationed at a given entrance is corrupt. I feel good about our security for the short term."

She looked at him with renewed respect. "You've had some experience with this sort of thing."

Cael crossed one booted foot over the other. "Five years."

"And before that." She didn't know what made her continue to press. "Navy SEALs or Marine Recon?" There was a flicker in his eyes, his only reaction. "Could be Rangers, I suppose, although you don't strike me as the army type."

"Thank God for that," he said feelingly. "I was navy for twelve years. A SEAL for ten."

She nodded, ridiculously pleased that she'd guessed correctly. His training showed. And he looked far more at home in

the black khakis and matching polo shirt he wore than he had
in the suit he'd worn in Metro City. He'd look even more natural
in combat fatigues, face smeared with camo paint. There were
some men who never lost the edge acquired in active duty. On
Cael McCabe, she had a feeling that edge went bone deep.

When his look turned appraising she had to suppress the
urge to fidget like a schoolgirl. "So my background's an open
book. You're more difficult to read. You didn't acquire your
marksmanship in the military."

Wariness reared, an innate defense whenever conversation turned personal. "No." Moments passed and it was
apparent that her answer hadn't appeased his curiosity appreciably. So she gave him a carefully edited form of the truth.
"I learned from my dad. He had me shooting by the time I
was six. Competing at ten." Her skill had been the only thing
that had ever won his approval. An approval that had been just
as quickly withdrawn a few years later. Forever.

"Let me guess." A corner of his mouth curled. "He
wanted a son."

There was a kick in her chest at the accuracy of his words.
Funny how even a sliver of the truth could still sting, after all
these years. She hadn't seen her father since before Alex was
born, at his insistence. It was shaming to recall how long it
had taken her to realize that was for the best.

"He wanted someone other than me." The note of finality
in her tone was meant to close the subject. She'd already
shared far more than she had with most people. The past
could only trip her up. Slow her down. She lived her life in
the present. Alex. Her job. Her friends. Most of the time—
almost always—it was enough.

His half smile faded. "Yeah." There was a note of something unidentifiable in his tone. "I have a father like that
myself." Now he was the one who seemed eager to change the
subject. Pushing away from the doorjamb, he half turned to
view her bedroom through the open doorway and stilled.

Wondering at his reaction, she peered around his shoulder, scanned the room again.

It was unmistakably a woman's space. The marble floors were smudged with light rose, the walls blushed with the same color. The drapes had been pulled away from the windows so the sheers moved lazily in the air stirred by a trio of overhead fans. The furniture was feminine and fussy, with lots of dark wood and carving, all balanced on delicate legs.

There were more sheers surrounding the enormous four-poster bed. And once her attention turned to it, she, too, stared, nonplussed.

It was more like a lake than a bed, far larger than any standard size. It was covered in shimmering silk the color of the pale turquoise waters that edged the San Baltes shores. There were throw pillows the size of couch cushions arranged invitingly along its headboard. Gilted mirrors lined the ceiling above the bed, faithfully reflecting the surface beneath. Her bag sat on the rug beside the bed, looking utilitarian and out of place.

It was a room meant for a woman, but one used for entertaining a man. Ava wondered for the first time at the age of the building, and the occupants the room had been meant to house. It looked like the place the earlier dictator would have stashed his mistress, while he slept overhead with his wife and children. She turned to say as much to Cael, but found his gaze on her, alight with intensity. And the words slid down her throat, unuttered.

She'd seen his expression shrewd. Grim. But she'd never seen arousal there, though it was instantly recognizable now. The skin pulled tightly across his cheekbones and his mouth looked fuller somehow. More sensual. And the glint in his pale green eyes was predatory and intimate at once.

A silent moment stretched, a thrumming beat filled with a single unspoken thought. Images swarmed her mind, sexual and stimulating. Of bodies pressed against each other on the silk, limbs entwined, the reflection of flesh on flesh replicating the sensual scene. A visual echo of every touch. Each stroke and kiss. Enveloping the couple on the bed in a cocoon of intimacy.

She saw his gaze go past her, linger on that bed for a long instant before returning to her. She read his intent in his eyes. The slow descent of his mouth toward hers gave her plenty of time to move away. To say something to break the moment.

She did neither. Instead she closed that last small space between their lips and tasted him.

His hand snaked out to cup her nape, to urge her closer while his mouth twisted over hers. There was nothing tentative about his kiss. It was bold and compelling, much like the man himself. His tongue pressed her lips apart and swept into her mouth as if staking a claim. She pressed a bit closer and answered his unspoken demand with one of her own.

Her job often called for subterfuge. Hiding her past certainly did. Which was why she tried to be frankly honest in the rest of her life. So she didn't try to hide the heat that balled in the pit of her belly, rocketing through her system with tiny spirals of fire. She savored his flavor, rife with sexual promise. Even as she knew she'd never allow that promise to come to fruition.

His taste was darkly sensual, and it was all too easy to imagine the two of them moving just a few more yards to the bed a slight distance away, silent and beckoning. To unleash the desire sprinting through her veins and ride the passion until they were both spent and weak.

Just the glimmer of the idea was terrifying. Especially with this man. Under these circumstances. She was shocked at the totally inappropriateness of her reaction. She hadn't allowed her hormones to rule her common sense in over fifteen years. And there was too much at stake to do so now.

But there was a tiny part of her that was elated at the evidence that her sexuality wasn't dead after all. Just buried and dormant. And apparently just waiting to spring forth at the least suitable moment.

Appalled by the totally inappropriate direction of her thoughts, Ava broke the connection by stepping away. Taking a few paces into the room, she strove for steadiness, attempting to rein in her pulse that still rollicked like a runaway mare. "It's a little fussier than I'm used to, but I'm not inclined to be picky about where I sleep at this point. Even the boardroom was beginning to look good to me earlier."

There was a moment of silence, as if Cael was having difficulty deciding whether to follow her into normalcy or pull her back in his arms and convincing her to let passion rule.

And when his voice sounded normal behind her, she was contrary enough, female enough, to mourn, just a little. "You're on at seven a.m. Radio Benton and see where to meet them. I don't know how early a riser de la Reyes will be now that he's returned home. I'll hold briefings twice a day about the investigation, so you'll be updated sometime tomorrow evening. Wear a vest over your clothes. The vest and radio will be delivered to your room before you leave your shift."

She turned to look at him, and her lack of enthusiasm must have shown in her expression, because he said firmly, "Yeah, in this heat it's going to be uncomfortable, but wearing a vest is nonnegotiable when you're on duty. I'm going to make damn sure you make it safely back to Metro City."

His concern for her managed to strengthen the blade of guilt that refused to dissipate. A guilt that had no validity. She had every intention of earning every dollar of the outrageous salary he was paying her. She could do the job for him and still provide a full report to Samuelson. The two tasks weren't mutually exclusive.

When an inner voice jeered at the thought, she squelched it firmly. "I'll wear the vest, of course. But I'll make it safely home because I'm a professional. I know how to do my job."

"If you didn't you wouldn't be here." Cael reached for the knob. And she knew enough about men to recognize the source of the regret in his expression. "Lock your door, Ava."

He closed it behind him with a quiet *snick*. But for a moment she stood, transfixed. Surely it must be lack of sleep that had her senses so highly attuned. She was used to intercepting and deflecting male interest. She wasn't used to responding to it. Not in a very long time.

Jerkily, she moved to the door, secured it. It was merely a security precaution. Logically she knew that. They were in an unfamiliar country, surrounded by strangers, any one of whom might be willing to betray their client for the right price. There was no reason, none at all, to believe that Cael had had another meaning for the warning.

Like locking the door against *him*.

She quickly unpacked, neatly placing her meager belongings in drawers in the fancy bureau. Her toiletries sat atop a marbled vanity in the adjoining bathroom, looking functional and forlorn amidst the scroll and gilt that adorned the mirrors above the counter. Ava had never stayed in a room more destined to make her aware of her own femininity. It was fortunate she wouldn't be spending much time in it.

She brushed her teeth, then swiftly changed into a camisole and loose-fitting pajama shorts. It wouldn't do to recall just how much a woman she'd felt only moments earlier. When she'd read the desire on Cael McCabe's face. Felt a matching emotion. She'd barely dated since her divorce; hadn't even missed it. But McCabe called to all sorts of long-buried feelings in her, and none of them had anything remotely in common with "dating."

Padding back into the bedroom, she crossed to the bed and pulled back the silk comforter. Spying her empty luggage next to the dresser, she paused, recalling the camera pen she'd packed in it. It was probably as safe there as it would be anywhere in the room. But it would be safer still, not to mention more useful, if she concealed it on her person.

She went and picked up the bag and brought it back across the room. Not for the first time she wished she'd shunned the damn thing, along with all the other espionage gadgets Samuelson had tried to press on her. As if by doing so she could negate the vague feeling of disloyalty she felt to McCabe for her dual purpose here.

Unzipping the side compartment on the bag, she thrust her hand inside, brought out the notepad. With a hiss of frustration she tried again, her fingers searching the space. Ava's breathing hitched. Frantically, she pulled the luggage onto her lap so she could spread the pocket wide and peer inside.

It was empty.

The high-tech camera pen was missing. Her shoulders slumped as her mind raced. There were only a few plausible scenarios.

But she was betting on the one where it ended up in McCabe's hands.

Chapter 4

Cael leaned on the balcony railing as he stared out into the star-studded night, speaking on his cell to Reynolds. "Do it, then. But I'd feel better if you didn't go alone."

"This guy's greedy but not totally stupid. He'll show me the way to the jungle camp, but he's afraid of Ramirez. Most people around here are. I don't want to scare him off by bringing someone else along."

"Did you suggest a flyover?"

"He's okay with that, but from what he describes of the camp's whereabouts, I think it's unlikely we'd be able to see anything from the air."

Unsurprised, Cael nodded. That kind of camouflage would be exactly what would have led the rebels to hide the camps in the jungle to begin with. They'd carve out a space with machetes, leaving enough of the natural vegetation to still blend in with their surroundings, set up shop for a few weeks, and then move on to another spot. Within a few weeks, the jungle's encroachment would fill in the deserted camps, making them virtually undetectable again.

"Go ahead and set it up. I'll run it by de la Reyes in the morning, but I'm confident he'll be intrigued enough at the prospect that he'll authorize the payment. Just watch your back." It would take a tough individual to believe he could double-cross Reynolds, although Cael was more worried about the guy leading his man into an ambush. But he had enough confidence in Reynolds to know the man could take care of himself. The opportunity for intelligence gathering more than offset the danger.

When the conversation ended, Cael slipped the cell in his pants pocket and stripped his shirt over his head, laying it across the railing. He didn't move to reenter the bedroom. He wouldn't be able to sleep. Not when he was still feeling this restless.

He leaned his forearms on the railing, broodingly surveying the manicured grounds below. There were lots of details still to be ironed out. Variables to be examined and weighed as he sifted through options. But it wasn't the particulars of the job his mind was occupied with. It was the woman down the hall.

He hauled in a breath, caught the scent from the gardens below. And that, too, reminded him of Ava.

Touching her had been a mistake. A pleasurable one, to be sure, but a mistake all the same. He didn't mix business with pleasure. Not ever. Especially with a woman in his employ. One he wasn't even sure he could trust.

He'd never had a problem compartmentalizing before, adhering to that line that separated the professional from the personal. Granted, females were in a minority in his profession. Amelia Driscoll was the only woman he had on staff, but he trusted her instincts as much as he did any of his male operatives. Of course, Amelia had the voice and build of a drill sergeant, so his strictly business relationship with her wasn't exactly proof of his lack of bias.

He'd have to be dead not to notice Ava's looks, but it was

her skill that had led to his initial job offer. That had him setting aside paranoia and allowing her on the team, hedging his bets. If she had nothing to do with Samuelson, he was ahead one solid team member. If she was linked to the man, she was a valuable pawn to be used in the bitter game between Cael and the DHS agent.

He wouldn't hesitate to use any man who planned to double-cross him in just that way. So it was particularly discomfiting to identify the emotion swirling through him now.

Guilt. He moved his shoulders uncomfortably. He had no reason to feel guilty. If Ava was blameless, she'd never have to know the suspicion that he'd harbored even as he'd reached for her. Tasted her.

And if she wasn't blameless…he felt something inside him harden. Then God have mercy on her, because he'd show her none.

The slight breeze cooled his skin, which seemed heated and much too tight. It was time to quit kidding himself. His reaction to Ava Carter had nothing to do with the job. She was a woman he could admire physically and professionally, and that alone made her dangerous. Add in the fact that he actually *liked* her, liked her attitude, and her wariness and the intriguing hint of vulnerability she'd displayed earlier, and the caution flags were impossible to ignore.

It wasn't smart to take unnecessary risks in his line of work, where lives often hung in the balance. And it'd be hazardous indeed to get involved with Ava. How hazardous he didn't yet know.

Broodingly, he rested more of his weight against the railing, his gaze blind to the lights winking in the far-off distance. To the swoop of the bats as they pursued their evening meal.

The only image he saw was that of long dark hair and pale slender limbs against a turquoise pool of silk. Heat flooded his belly at the mental picture.

He wasn't a man ruled by his hormones. The folly of that path had been painfully learned his seventeenth year when Liza Watkin's father's descent into the basement had outpaced Cael's dexterity with his zipper. Patience and timing always paid off in the long run.

But he could know that, accept it and still stand here wishing he hadn't urged Ava Carter to lock her door.

A tiny sound pricked the deep cocoon of Ava's unconscious. She fought the binds of sleep sluggishly. It had been hours before she dropped off, and now slumber tugged at her with tiny anchors, slowing her return to awareness.

Then she felt heaviness settle over her, felt an all too human heat transfer to her skin, and instinct slugged through unconsciousness.

One hand shot out and up, made contact with flesh and cartilage. She heard a muffled grunt of pain even as she came fully awake, her other hand going unerringly for an eye gouge.

She was pinned more securely, a heavy weight distributed over her as the man above her battled to grip her hands. And when her eyes flew open, adjusted to the dim early morning light, her body went completely still.

Cael McCabe stared down at her, his expression menacing. His nose was already red and swelling.

"What are you doing in here?" she hissed, disbelief mingling with embarrassment. She heaved under him attempting, with a notable lack of success, to dislodge him.

"Getting the hell beat out of me, apparently."

She stared at him, struggling to shake off the sleep-induced cobwebs. He was already dressed, if you could call it that. A black ribbed undershirt clung to his well-defined torso and was tucked into army-green khakis. The shirt left his shoulders and arms bare, and she was supremely aware of the bulk of them, as he lay stretched out atop her. He was unshaven, his dark blond hair still mussed as if he'd been roused by a matter of some urgency.

"Is it de la Reyes?" she demanded. "Has there been a breach in the security?"

"You could say that."

She stilled, searching his face carefully for his meaning. His eye color was even more startling up close, their pale green a near match for her August birthstone, the name of which she could never recall. She had the belated observation that he'd managed to get a haircut before he'd left the States, although he didn't wear it military short, as some of his men did.

And that his position was far too intimate. Hers far too vulnerable. He had her arms stretched out above her head, caught in one hand so she couldn't follow through with instinct and blind him before she'd figured out who it was. Now that she had she was all too conscious that the sheet was bunched at her waist. And although the camisole covered her decently, she was still far too bare to appear before a man who was her employer.

Especially this man.

Ava tugged ineffectually at her wrists. "You can let me go," she said stiffly. Tiny needles of alarm were firing through her veins, but she fought against revealing the emotion. "Sorry about the punch earlier, but it would have been safer all around to just knock." Even as she had the thought, her gaze flew over his shoulder to the door behind him. The dead bolt was still engaged. So he hadn't come in through the door. And he'd yet to release her hands. "Mind telling me how you got in here?"

"Turns out we have adjoining balconies."

Her eyes narrowed. "No. We don't. The nearest balcony is a good five yards away." She knew because she'd checked before making the decision to leave one balcony door open to catch the fresh night breeze.

Although his lips curved, they didn't soften appreciably. "True. But it also turns out that I'm blessed with catlike dexterity and reflexes." His voice went lower as he bent his head closer to hers, close enough that she could feel the slight abrasion of whiskers against her jaw. "Some men might construe an open door as an invitation, Ava." His barely discernible drawl had grown thicker. "Were you issuing an invitation?"

A quick shiver shimmied down her spine and warmth flushed her system. She was certain he could feel it. "No. A man in your occupation knows there's always more than one way to read a situation."

His head lifted and the glint in his eye had tension shooting through her muscles. "I do." He gave a slow nod. "I surely do." Reaching down with one hand, he withdrew something from his pants pocket and held it up so she could see it. "So I'm real interested to hear your explanation for this."

A boulder lodged in her throat. He was holding the camera pen. The one Samuelson had pressed on her. The one she'd discovered missing from her luggage last night.

It took all her effort to manufacture a neutral tone. "You're here because you found a pen?"

He cocked his head. "It's all in the details, isn't it? I'm here because *this* pen was found in *your* luggage. Hell, I'm here because this is more than a pen, isn't it?" With a flip of his thumb he clicked the stem and held the pen perpendicular to her face. One more click had a tiny light winking at her as the camera engaged.

He shoved his face closer to hers, his expression forbidding. "I'm here because I'm real interested in how you happen to possess a costly little gadget that's a couple generations removed from what's available on the market right now. So start talking, Ava. Because my read of the situation is pretty ugly."

When she remained silent, his mouth twisted. "Although I haven't heard of it, I suppose it's possible this little item is available on the black market. Trouble with that theory is I can't see you buying anything that way. Too much a law-and-order kind of gal, aren't you, Ava?"

She swallowed hard, wondering what he'd think if he realized her embrace of the justice system came relatively late in her life.

He gave her a shake, the look in his eyes lethal. "Let's stop dicking around. Samuelson approached you?"

She tried again to wrench her hands free, temper spiking when his one-handed grip held. The accuracy of his guess was surprising, but there was no use lying to him, at this point. "Paulus and Samuelson."

A terrible stillness came over him at her affirmation. Seeing it, Ava was struck anew by the awful certainty that there was much much more to this assignment than DHS had bothered to reveal to her.

Because fury pumped off him in waves, the strength of which surrounded her. Squeezed her in an unforgiving vise. It was several moments before he spoke again. And she knew the effort it took for him to keep the judgment from his voice. "So what'd they offer you?"

Disconcerted, she shook her head. "Nothing."

"Threaten you with, then. That's Samuelson's game, anyway. What'd he have on you?"

Ava hesitated. Honesty only went so far. She was unwilling to dredge up her past in an effort to pacify McCabe. She doubted it would make a difference to him anyway.

"He appealed to my sense of patriotism," she said carefully. "He wanted information on the stability of this government and I agreed that I could supply it without compromising my assignment here. I still believe that."

His mouth twisted. "You still believe that, huh? You know what I believe?" He reached over to hook a finger in the thin strap of her camisole, and urge it slowly, inexorably over her shoulder. One tiny expanse of skin at a time. "I believe that you can tell a person's honor in what they do when they don't think anyone will find out." His meaning slipped neatly between her ribs, like a well-placed blade. With a crooked knuckle, he caressed the skin he bared, and she flinched, feeling cheap and humiliated.

"I believe," he continued, his voice going lower, rougher, "that a person who will betray me in one area will betray me in all. That little lesson came later in life but it left its mark."

His free hand slid up the column of her throat, cupped her chin, his grip just shy of cruel. "And I believe you made the biggest mistake in your life to throw in with Samuelson, Ava Carter. One that's going to cost you dearly."

A trickle of fear crept up her spine, though she refused to lower her gaze. Too late to worry that she didn't know this man; couldn't guess what experiences had forged him, or how far he'd go to achieve his ends.

But from the ruthless expression on his face, she knew she was going to find out.

"Aren't you being a little melodramatic?" She jerked her face away from his grasp, suddenly angry at her position. If the agent had allowed her to do this her way, de la Reyes would remain safe, Samuelson would have been provided with the information he wanted and McCabe would be none the wiser. She'd only be wrestling with her conscience, not with one hundred ninety pounds of mean, furious ex-SEAL.

"Your commitment to your client's privacy is commendable. And I don't blame you for being angry with me." Anger was too tame a word for the dangerous look in those pale green eyes. A look that was a decided contrast to the expression in them the last time they'd been together in this room. "But my providing Samuelson information about the political climate here is hardly going to endanger de la Reyes, or detract from the protection we're providing him."

The smile that curled one corner of his mouth then was derisive. "Is that what he told you? That he was concerned about the political climate in San Baltes? Either you're unbelievably gullible or you think I am. The U.S. has ignored San Baltes for decades. And now all of a sudden they're so concerned they require a covert spy operation consisting of one lone police officer from no-name, California?"

His words had the unease that had lingered in her belly since Samuelson's visit congealing into a hard knot of dread. Stubbornly, she refused to concede his point. "We're talking about DHS here. It's not beyond plausibility that they'd want to grab every opportunity to extract information, especially in a way that costs them nothing and doesn't lead back to them."

"It's not DHS, it's Samuelson," he corrected. "You remember him. Tall, humorless prick with a bad comb-over? Where he's concerned nothing is plausible, least of all his word. Face it, you were duped, Ava. He didn't urge you down here to get information on San Baltes, de la Reyes or the political climate. He sent you to get information on *me*."

Shocked, she regarded him with wide eyes, her mind racing furiously. But the more frantically it reached for answers, the less any of them made sense. "You're paranoid," she said finally.

"You know what they say." His voice had gone lower. Raspier. "Just because you're paranoid doesn't mean people aren't out to get you."

What the hell had she gotten herself entangled in? she wondered wildly. Some vendetta between a DHS agent and McCabe? Or was this man a raving lunatic?

She eyed him carefully. His face was all harsh angles in the early morning shadows, but his expression was determined. Whatever he was saying, he believed implicitly, even if he'd left out as much from his story as Samuelson had.

Silence stretched between them. He studied her from beneath lowered lids, and she became supremely conscious of the weight of him, the heat as she lay stretched out beneath him. Her lungs felt strangled. Last night she'd grappled with fragmented dreams, too similar to this moment for comfort.

But in the dreams their struggle on this bed ended much differently. And the memory of those unconscious snippets had her face burning.

"Get off me." She arched beneath him, the vulnerability of her position stinging. "I'm not having this conversation with a two-ton ex-military ape crushing me."

His fingers clasped her face and he sent a thumb skating across her lips. "Ava. Do you really think you're in the position to be giving orders here?"

"Perhaps not." She aimed a lethal stare at him. "But if I were you I'd start worrying about what I'll do when I'm no longer in this position."

"Threats." A thread of admiration entered his tone. "I was right about your guts at least, if nothing else."

She didn't respond. Because it was appearing all too clear that she'd been right about very little ever since meeting the man.

His heart thudded against hers, as if in an answering tattoo. He shifted infinitesimally and she went still. His shoulders blocked out the early morning light spilling into the room through the double doors he'd left open. His chest was broad and his biceps bulged with muscles. But it was the change in his expression that had the breath catching in her throat. That instant when temper and resolve were replaced by something much more primitive. Something that had flickers of heat igniting in her veins.

Their gazes melded and for one second all thought vanished. And that was perhaps the most dangerous moment of all.

In the next instant he rolled off her, with a suddenness that was disconcerting. "Get dressed," he rasped, rapidly crossing to the door. "We'll finish this in my office in ten minutes."

It was closer to a half hour before Ava stepped inside the boardroom turned command center. Cael felt her presence before he heard her enter. And that sensitivity, that awareness of her left him edgy.

"This is the president's final schedule for the day?" It took more effort than it should have to return his focus to Benton. It was his operative who had brought him the device found in Ava's bag. The device that had removed all doubt about the woman's reason for coming here.

Recalling it now had his stomach burning. Because even with the bitter sense of betrayal blooming fresh and raw inside him, he'd still reacted to her. His body had responded to the woman rather than the employee set to betray him. It wouldn't be the first time he'd given the benefit of the doubt to the wrong person.

But it would be the last time he made that mistake with Ava Carter.

He flicked a glance at Benton. "Thanks for bringing me this. As long as you've got Sibbits covering for you now, it's your turn to sleep."

The man looked at Ava, back again. "I can pull a double shift, Cael. Maybe between Sibbits and me—"

"That won't be necessary." He aimed a chilly smile at the woman in the doorway. "Ava is capable of pulling her weight here. As a matter of fact, she was quite convincing earlier today when she assured me of just that."

There was pleasure in watching her creamy skin flush, twin patches of color coming, then going in her cheeks. But her voice as she strolled into the room was maddenly nonchalant. "What happened to your face? Looks like someone slipped under your famed guard and clipped you a good one."

He touched his nose, which was more sore than he'd admit. He owed her for that. Owed her for far more, apparently. But her bravado sparked a sense of exhilaration. Damned if he didn't find it stimulating to spar with her. Unfortunately he found her stimulating in more ways than one.

He'd chosen the location of their prior skirmish poorly. He

could acknowledge that now, with the memory of her long, lean curves branded on his skin. Her scent emblazoned on his senses. But his body's reaction to her would have no bearing on the end result of their relationship. He'd make certain of that.

"You'll find that once my guard is breached I'm less trusting the next time." He was only half aware of Benton slipping out the door unnoticed, closing the door behind him.

She halted across the table from him, her hands resting lightly on the chair back. "It's encouraging to hear you tell Benton I'll be going on duty. We both know you can ill-afford to lose an operative right now. You need my skills and you need the extra manpower I provide. I'm not a threat to de le Reyes or to you. And whatever is going on between Agent Samuelson and you, I want no part of it."

Just the mention of the man's name shot Cael with a familiar bitter resolve. "Unfortunately, you've become central to what's between Samuelson and me." He gave a careless shrug. "Hard to work up much sympathy for you, in light of the circumstances. You came down here to gather information for the bastard, and you'll do just that. But I'll be the one to determine what information you deliver to him."

She gave a slight shake to her head. "What's your story? I can believe he left out a lot—a helluva lot—from the tale he wove for me, but he's a fed." Information was shared on a need-to-know basis, and according to most feds, there was damn little local law enforcement needed to know. "But if you believe he wanted me here because of you there must be a lot of history between the two of you. I deserve to know what that entails."

He tossed de la Reyes's schedule carelessly on the table. "Sure you want to get into what you *deserve*, Ava?" A moment passed and when she didn't rise to the bait, he lifted a shoulder. "We have a history, yeah. He hates my guts. I return the emotion, in spades. He'd like to see me dead. I'll settle for seeing him ruined." Flattening his palms on the table, he leaned forward, a measure of the satisfaction curling through him sounding in his voice.

"And you, Ava, are going to be the tool I use to make that happen."

Chapter 5

Their gazes clashed. Not a flicker of emotion crossed Ava's face, and Cael felt an unwilling tug of admiration. Sheer guts and skill wrapped up in a stunning package. It was too bad she'd had the damned poor judgment to throw in with Samuelson.

"I'm no one's *tool*," she said with heavy emphasis. "I don't know what's going on between the two of you, but I'm taking myself out of the equation."

He wondered if she realized the defiance in her tone was a dare. One that he was tempted, very tempted, to take her up on. "Oh, you're very much in the equation," he murmured. "Too much so for my peace of mind. You placed yourself right in the center of things." Fury looked good on her, he observed. Brought color to her cheeks and dangerous lights to those dark eyes.

"I'm not a pawn to be moved at will by you or your personal nemesis. So whatever game you're engaged in with Samuelson, you'll play it alone." Shoving away from the table, she walked to the door, spine straight.

And he let her go. There was nothing more to be discussed, at any rate. Ava Carter wasn't a woman who'd bend easily to a man's will. If she was telling the truth about her involvement with Samuelson, a big *if,* he reminded himself grimly, maybe she'd agreed out of a sense of duty to her country.

He considered that, his hands gripping and releasing the chair back as he regarded the door she'd closed behind her. He doubted the agent had offered her money. He was a shady son of a bitch, but he wouldn't dare leave a paper trail like that for his superiors to follow. No, he'd tried something else. Manipulative prick that he was, he'd try appealing to her patriotism or blackmail. He'd used similar methods with Cael over the years.

Moodily, he mulled over the possibilities. But the truth was staring him right in the face.

He'd never seen a woman more difficult to manipulate than Ava Carter. That left blackmail, or something like it. A woman like her would have few weaknesses, other than her son, of course.

Cael pulled his cell phone out of his pocket and pressed the number for the information broker he used on a regular basis. Something had to exist in Ava's life that he could use as leverage.

And whatever it was, he was going to discover it.

Then he was going to use it to acquire her cooperation to bring down Samuelson, once and for all.

Two things became very clear throughout the day Ava spent at de la Reyes's side. One was that he was an extremely busy man. He went from meeting to meeting, briefing to briefing, phone call to phone call with barely a moment to himself.

The second was that her presence, and that of the rest of McCabe's team, was fiercely resented by the palace guard. She imagined imprisoning their leader, Gonzalez, had been the first indignity. The next had been disarming some of them.

Ten national guardsmen were part of the president's protection contingent. And for the first time in her life, Ava
wished she weren't bilingual. Because her language skills
meant she could easily interpret the whispered grumbles of
the men surrounding her. The asides that grew increasingly
personal. Especially when she, on more than one occasion,
inserted herself before a guardsman to maintain her position
by the president's side at all times. Or when they were closed
out of a private meeting with the president and one of his
cabinet members, while she remained in the room.

She wondered why the nationals really expected that she'd
be unable to understand their remarks. The term *puta* was,
after all, pretty universally understood. So perhaps they didn't
much care whether she spoke their language or not.

Because it would do no good to let on otherwise, she
stood stoically through all the undertone conversations.
Ignored the snippets of disparaging comments that drifted
her way. And seethed silently when a couple of the guards
discussed her physical attributes at length. And what they
were better suited for.

The only positive note was that the frustration she felt
was an admirable distraction from the earlier conversations
with McCabe.

It would be more comfortable to regard the man as an
oversuspicious zealot. But she shared his dim opinion of Samuelson. Had distrusted the man from the first. And could
admit now how effortlessly the man had manipulated her.
He'd discovered just enough about her to know what button
to push; then he'd played her like a master.

And the bitterness accompanying that realization burned
as much as McCabe's opinion of her did.

The problems with secrets was that they left one vulnerable. She shifted position and pretended not to hear the
comments about the shape of her ass. She may well have
decided to join McCabe's operatives anyway, given her

sudden need of cash. But it had been her hunger to keep her past from crashing into her present that had cemented her decision, and it was easy to see what a mistake in judgment that had been.

One thing she was determined of—she wasn't going to let McCabe use her to deceive DHS Agent Samuelson. Whatever was going on between the two men would unfold without her. She'd failed to convince him of that earlier today, so she'd gone on duty with their argument unresolved. But she wasn't going to be the match that lit the fuse between them.

She shoved the troublesome thoughts away to concentrate on the three cabinet members currently meeting with de la Reyes. All had been searched, of course. But it was also her job to weigh and evaluate them for personal threat. Each had expressed horror at the president's near death in the States. Apparently the attempt on the man's life yesterday had been kept quiet. Probably McCabe's doing. None of the president's visitors today had mentioned it.

The conversation had turned to efforts to curb criminal elements in the country, and a familiar name was mentioned.

"We've intercepted and jailed a dozen more couriers we suspect work for Ramirez," Emanuel Ortega, head of Justicia, was reporting in Spanish. "We continue to strangle his ability to conduct his business."

"And what of his assets?" Antonio de la Reyes looked at a second man, his director of International Finance. "I want him stopped. To do so we must cripple him where it hurts him the most."

Ramon Jorge inclined his head. He was a wizened little man, the wrinkles in his face giving him a raisinlike appearance. "We've located the blind trusts he's using and put a stop to the offshore banking he was engaged in. His assets have been frozen."

De la Reyes slapped his palm on the polished teak table. "Excellent." Satisfaction laced his tone. "We can expect that to draw him out, if nothing else. Without ready cash, he'll become increasingly desperate."

The men exchanged glances, and Ava knew intuitively what they were thinking. A desperate man was increasingly dangerous. If Ramirez had anything to do with the attempts on the president's life, his survival had just gotten more precarious.

And their job here had become even more difficult.

It was later in the afternoon, during de la Reyes's meeting with the archbishop of his church, that the guardsmen on duty with her changed tactics, grew bolder.

The first brush of a body against hers had Ava shifting slightly. The second time it happened was harder to ignore. Especially when she turned to catch the smirk on the guardsman's face closest to her. She waited, teeth gritted, for his palm to move over her backside once more, then, eyes still straight ahead, snaked a hand behind to catch the marauding palm. With a quick practiced move she wrenched it up and back, surprising a muffled yelp from the guardsman.

The meeting room went silent. The archbishop sent an inquiring look their way and de la Reyes aimed a glare that encompassed the entire team. The man in back of Ava shuffled his feet and muttered an apology for the interruption. A moment later the president resumed the meeting. And the men surrounding her gave her plenty of room without crowding her for the duration.

The meetings lasted until well after five o'clock that evening, when the last visitor left and de la Reyes headed to his quarters to change prior to the evening meal. Sibbits was waiting outside the conference room with a new team of guardsmen. With a cursory nod toward Ava, he fell into step behind de la Reyes and strode out the door.

The National Guardsmen on her detail headed toward the door until her voice stopped them. *"Para a la derecha allí. Quiero una palabra con usted."*

Under any other circumstances, the men's reaction to her command, uttered in flawless Spanish, would have been comical. Ava's sense of humor, however, had vanished somewhere between *puta* and that hand on her ass.

She waited until she had their attention and continued on in their native tongue. "If today was an example of the way you do your job, I can guarantee that you will not remain employed much longer. I could round up a gang of ten-year-olds more professional than the bunch of you." Some of the men shot looks at each other, but all remained silent. Her voice grew more contemptuous. "Your antics were juvenile and distracting at a time where your caution should be at its highest point. You'd better report for shift tomorrow and impress me with your expertise or you'll all be looking for new jobs. Understand?"

Surprise had turned to sullenness on the men's faces after her spate of scathing Spanish. But there were enough muttered *"entendido"*s to satisfy her. She waited for the first of them to reach the door before adding, "Oh, and the next one who touches me? *I' rotura del ll su brazo maldito.*"

Her threat, delivered in as sunny a tone as she could manage, had a few of the guards exchanging glances, but all were silent as they trooped out.

Ava released a long hissed breath and worked her shoulders to release the tension of the day. Then felt that tension ratchet up again when Cael came striding into the room.

The long hours since their argument this morning vanished. Trepidation mingled with resolve. If he were here to start up where they left off this morning, he'd find her unswerved. Regardless of what he had in mind, there was no way he could force her into this unhealthy contention between him and the DHS agent.

But telling herself that didn't vanquish the trepidation curling in her stomach.

However, his words had nothing to do with their earlier

conversation. "I've got Perez and Reynolds in the field. I'll need you to take a shift at Gonzalez's quarters until Perez gets back in."

Shrugging off weariness, Ava agreed immediately. "All right. Where's he being held?"

"I'll show you." Cael waited for her to cross the room and closed the door behind her, before leading her through the halls toward an exit.

"I'll have a meal sent out, of course. Perez won't be back until late, so I'll spell you in a few hours."

"The head of Justicia told de la Reyes they've frozen Ramirez's assets."

Cael nodded. His stride was long, but she easily kept up with him as they made their way through the wending hallways. "I met with him after the meeting. His forensic analysts also have determined that a large unexplained deposit was made into both Cabrerra's and Gonzalez's account late last week."

Ava looked at him, adrenaline spiking. "While de la Reyes was in the States."

"That's right." Cael's frustration was apparent. "He's given us nothing so far, but I'm looking forward to hitting him with this new evidence and seeing if he gets more talkative. I don't want to trust any of his own men with the translation, though, so it'll have to wait until Perez or Reynolds gets back."

"I can translate." The offer was out of her mouth before she even took the time to consider it. But she found herself as eager as Cael to take the investigation to the next level and determine if Cabrerra's superior was as dirty as he'd been.

"You're bilingual?"

"As inconvenient as that turned out to be today," she said dryly, "I am. Fluent enough to translate if you want to interrogate the chief of the National Guard right now."

He'd stopped in his tracks and was studying her speculatively. "You seem to have all sorts of hidden talents, Ava." But his tone was anything but admiring.

Annoyed, she shrugged. "Or you can wait for Perez. It doesn't matter to me."

"I'd rather do it now." He still hadn't moved, but she knew his mind was racing. "I'm not fluent enough to be sure I'm making myself understood, especially to elicit the kind of details we're looking for." He was silent for a moment, regarding her with his piercing gaze. He'd pulled a shirt on over the ribbed undershirt he'd appeared in at dawn, and it matched the green fatigues he wore. The hue made his eye color more striking, and noticing that annoyed her.

She was here to do a job. Responding to McCabe on any level was a diversion she could ill-afford. The lecture she'd leveled at the guardsmen earlier could just as easily be applied to her. Distractions put lives at risk.

And that was only one of the many reasons it was a mistake to respond to this man. On any level.

As if coming to a sudden decision, he said, "Let's do it." He was moving again and she remained silent as they wound their way through the different levels of security he'd established inside and outside the palace walls.

Acres of well-tended grounds surrounded the palatial structure. Cael strode to a jeep parked nearby and once she got in, drove well beyond the palace, through yet another gate in a decorative stone wall.

Ava saw what amounted to a small village. It was here that the help would live.

Cael's next words underscored her impression. "Cooks, housekeepers and gardeners stay here." He gestured to rows of attached apartments, each slightly larger than an American double garage. "Their schedule is a fourteen-six rotation. Two straight weeks of work, then six days free. Most of them travel some distance to get home and see their families. But the leave and pay are regarded as quite generous in this country."

The jeep bumped along the brick drive, painted a dull red. The apartments and curb were whitewashed, and everything looked neat and well tended, if lacking the jaw dropping landscaping of the main grounds. But it was another half mile before Cael pointed to row upon row of single-story structures, much larger than the two-tiered apartments.

"These house the palace guard. Gonzalez is in the back one that sits in the center."

Ava recognized Benton standing outside the structure with an AR-15 rifle strapped across his chest. A thought occurred. "I would imagine that putting their senior officer under house arrest didn't go over too well with the guardsmen." She could attest to her team's antipathy, at least. "What's to stop them from overpowering the guard and releasing their superior?"

"If they're loyal to de la Reyes that allegiance will outweigh their fidelity to Gonzalez."

He seemed to be skirting the obvious. "And if they're not?"

"Then we hope the explosives we wired to Gonzalez's quarters, in full sight of the guardsmen, will serve as adequate deterrent from any zealots intent on a rescue." Cael's grin was sharkish.

Remembering the weaponry and explosive devices in the back of the SUV they'd driven from the airport, Ava subsided. She had no doubt about his expertise with wiring and detonators. If he'd fitted Gonzalez's quarters with a combination of those, a rescue attempt would end up killing both the head of the palace guard, and the would-be rescuers.

It went without saying that whichever of Cael's operatives were standing guard would be dead first.

He pulled to a stop before the quarters and jumped out. Ava followed more slowly, as he engaged Benton in conversation. Walking up to the men, she saw the other operative flick her a glance and say, "Are you sure that's wise?"

Heat shot up her spine and she kept her expression carefully blank. He'd been the one to search her luggage, of course. The one to turn the camera over to his boss. And while McCabe had his own reasons for keeping her on here, it was clear that Benton didn't share them.

"I'm sure. Take the jeep and go get something to eat before grabbing some sleep. You'll be on de la Reyes again in a few hours."

The man wanted to argue. Ava could see that in his expression, which had suspicion flickering in it. But he was nothing if not well trained. Without another word he left them, climbed into the jeep and pulled away.

McCabe spent several moments keying in a code to the security keypad on the outside of the door. Then he took a bunch of keys from his pocket and inserted the proper one to unlock three different locks.

"Weapon ready."

Ava had her gun in her hand before the words even left his mouth. With a grim nod, he drew the sleek Luger from his shoulder holster and took up position at the other end of the doorway, swinging the door in.

When she followed him inside Ava saw a lone man, clad in undershirt, boxers and socks, seated in a leather recliner. If it weren't for the zip cord binding his ankles and wrists and the tether leading from them to a hook drilled into the plastered wall, he'd look like a middle-aged man relaxing on a weekend morning.

Of course, there was nothing relaxed about Rafael Gonzalez's expression. *"Hijo de Satan,"* the man spat. His look was venomous.

"Senor Gonzalez." Cael's voice was pleasant enough as he dragged a straight-backed chair out of the dining room to set it in front of the man. After gesturing Ava to it, he pulled another up for himself. "I understand you have been fed and given periodic restroom breaks, as per my instructions. Are there any medications you take regularly that we should be aware of?"

Ava repeated Cael's words in Spanish. The man's expression flickered a bit, but she thought it was in response to her command of his language rather than McCabe's inquiry about his well-being. He didn't appear to be a fan.

"Vaya al infierno."

Since the man's suggestion that Cael go to hell didn't appear to need a translation, Ava didn't offer one.

Gonzalez was barrel chested and thickly built, a powerful-looking man who should have appeared diminished by his position, but did not. He looked, she thought, pissed off and defiant. But not visibly frightened. He rattled off a spate of Spanish in a rush of angry words.

"He demands to know what you've done with President de la Reyes. He doesn't believe that the president ordered his imprisonment," Ava relayed.

"Maybe this will convince him." With his free hand, Cael extracted a folded sheet of paper with a seal on the back. He tossed it on the man's lap.

Gonzalez didn't so much as spare it a look. He never took his gaze off McCabe. "Tell him de la Reyes wrote the order for his imprisonment himself," Cael instructed. "The special seal is the one Gonzalez himself suggested used for times such as these to prove the missive isn't written under duress."

After Ava translated, the man's eyes lowered to the paper on his lap. It was tri-folded, like a letter. With his bound hands he clumsily turned it over, then stilled when he saw the seal securing it. And when he opened it, scanned the short message, he paled. Then he looked at Ava and spoke heatedly.

"He believes someone, probably you, has convinced the president of his guilt."

When she stopped then, Cael's brows rose. "I didn't catch all of it, but I know he said more."

She cocked a brow at him. "He also questioned your parentage, your manhood and sexual preference."

"Perhaps you'd like to address those last two issues with him," he murmured meaningfully.

Since the words were meant to embarrass her, she refused

to give him the satisfaction. "I can't say I have proof either way, so I'll pass."

"We could always rectify that," he suggested, ignoring Gonzalez for the moment. There was a light in his eyes, a dangerous heat. "What the hell, give you a bit more firsthand information to share with Samuelson."

"I can't imagine who'd be less impressed with that sort of information, Samuelson or me."

A corner of his mouth kicked up at that. But he said only, "Tell him we have proof he is working for Ramirez. That he's a traitor to his president. To his country."

When Ava obeyed, Gonzalez's reaction was fierce and immediate. When the man had halted his speech, trembling with fury, she translated, "You impugn his honor with your accusations. He has risked his life to keep the president safe. He wants to know what proof you could possibly have." She paused, smirking. "He also suggested that you spend your nights engaged in illicit activity with farm animals."

He slanted her a glance, the humor fading from his expression. "Let's keep the translation focused on the facts involving Gonzalez's involvement."

Her tone was innocent. "I thought you wanted to hear everything."

"I did. But you're enjoying this a bit too much." Withdrawing another paper from his shirt pocket, he handed it to Gonzalez. "Let him know that we have proof a large sum of money was deposited into his account recently. Ask him to deny that's his signature on the deposit slip."

Gonzalez made no move to unfold the paper until Ava had finished speaking. Then he opened it with the air of a man perusing his own death warrant. He shook his head violently, speaking to Ava in rapid Spanish.

"He says the signature looks like his but he did not sign such a slip. He denies all knowledge of it and claims someone is trying to make him look guilty." She paused while the man spoke again. "On the date listed on the slip, he was engaged in all-day training sessions with his men. He has hundreds of witnesses."

"And he must realize we know he didn't have to go to the bank himself to deposit that money. He could have filled out the slip and sent it along with someone else. Tell him to quit jerking me around." Cael's tone had grown hard. "If he has nothing else to share, he's wasting my time. I want information about the job Ramirez paid him for. The one he had Cabrerra try and carry out. What is Ramirez planning now that de la Reyes is back in the country?"

The man's protests to Ava's translation increased in volume. His black heavy mustache fairly quivered with outrage.

"He says one of Ramirez's men approached him once, not long after the election. He offered Gonzalez money—far more money than that deposit—to provide them with information regarding de la Reyes's security and schedule. Gonzalez says he refused. He suggests that perhaps they next approached Cabrerra with a similar offer."

"And that's where his story breaks down for me. Head of the president's security force and he didn't report the offer to de la Reyes? Did he tell anyone?"

Ava relayed Cael's questions, could tell Gonzalez's answer in the shift of his gaze from hers. His response was a long time coming.

"He says he was afraid telling de la Reyes he'd been approached would shake the president's faith in him. Perhaps regard him as a weak link in the security. He took efforts to warn his guard unit continually to report to him if they were contacted."

"Bullshit." Cael lurched from his chair, frustration rife in his movements. "So is that what Cabrerra did? Run to him and report that he'd accepted five thousand dollars to assassinate the San Baltes president when he was off-continent?

Because that's the amount we found in his account. Half what we found in Gonzalez's."

Her voice quiet, Ava leveled the questions in Spanish to the guard chief. The man only shook his head. He appeared smaller somehow since they'd started. As if the evidence against him and mention of his trusted second in command had carved away his defiance.

"No tenia ninguna idea que Cabrerra era corrupto. Habria estacado mi vida en su lealtad. Estaque el presidente vida de s en el. Y lo casi mataron consecuentemente."

"I had no idea that Cabrerra was corrupt," Ava translated softly. "I would have staked my life on his loyalty. I did stake the president's life on it. And he was almost killed as a result."

Cael stared hard at the man for a long moment. She wondered if he was as close to believing him as she was. The evidence against him looked damning. But it would be easy enough to forge a signature, wouldn't it? Especially with Cabrerra working so closely with the man. Simpler still to deposit money in an account to frame Gonzalez.

"We'll look at the security tapes for the day of the deposit," Cael said finally. "He remains in custody until we have positive proof of his innocence." He got up, leaving Ava to translate, and walked to the door.

She joined him outside and he reengaged the security system. "Anyone could have made that deposit to point suspicion toward Gonzalez." She holstered her weapon, although she kept the grip unsnapped.

"They could." He turned to regard her, his expression thoughtful. "But we're left with the question of why. Say Cabrerra had gotten away with the assassination. U.S. police would think the killer was one of the wackos who'd called in a death threat, or someone like them. There was no reason to point suspicion at Gonzalez. Not when Cabrerra also had a smaller deposit to his account. It makes them both look guilty."

"And muddies the waters for any investigation of their bank funds."

"I'd say they're sufficiently muddied at this point. He could also be a convincing liar, faced with evidence of his guilt, trying like hell to make it seem like Cabrerra was in on it by himself." He surprised her then by asking, "What's your read on him?"

"He was convincing," she admitted. Her gaze scanned the area around them, taking note of the off-duty guardsmen coming and going from their barracks. "But I'm stuck on the motivation issue, too. Ramirez might hate Gonzalez enough for turning him down that he wants to ruin him. But to what end? That money was put in their accounts while de la Reyes was still in America. The assassination hadn't yet gone wrong. Who did Ramirez think was going to look in the bank accounts and why bother when the plan was to make it look like an American citizen had killed the president?"

"It might have been blackmail, I suppose." Cael leaned against the doorjamb with a nonchalance that Ava didn't share. Call her paranoid, but she didn't intend to touch the house he'd wired with explosives unless absolutely necessary. "Maybe Ramirez was hedging his bets. If the assassination is successful, he's only out ten thousand dollars. If not, they could have been planning some way to cast suspicion on Gonzalez and away from a U.S. citizen. We may have even thwarted those plans by getting the forensic accounting done so quickly. De la Reyes would be persuaded to choose another chief of security."

"Maybe," she said. If there was another explanation for the deposit, it involved a plan they could only speculate on. It was far more likely that Gonzalez was as guilty as he looked, despite his convincing act earlier. "We can't afford to trust him at this point."

"Agreed. Trust is in short supply on this trip, at any rate." It wasn't so much the tone of his voice as the meaningful look in his eye.

"Something tells me you don't exactly overflow with the quality on the best of days." She was through feeling guilty for her duplicity. His motives in relation to Samuelson weren't exactly pure. "You know you and Samuelson have a lot in common." She didn't noticed the stillness that came over him at the words. Not then. "Both of you are bullies. Both will use your position to strong-arm people into giving you what you want. And both of you deserve to be taken down a notch."

"An interesting observation." The bleakness in his eyes stemmed the temper that had prompted her outburst. "But any similarities between us are purely coincidental."

Cael turned away as a thought hit him with a force that nearly sent him reeling. He and the DHS agent had been dancing around this antipathy for years. It had gotten steadily stronger on Cael's side with the man's consistent efforts to undermine him.

What if Samuelson knew him better than he thought? Ava might be more than the latest attempt to damage him and his credibility. Could Samuelson have sensed she was a woman he'd react to?

What if she'd been selected as the very personal weapon of Cael's destruction?

Chapter 6

Cael pored over the painstaking directions Reynolds had written down to the rebel camp, comparing them to the topographic map of the country.

"And you saw it for yourself? How many stationed there?"

"Hard to say," Reynolds responded laconically. "I counted over a hundred. But there's no way to be sure how many were inside the buildings." He leaned forward to point to a map he'd drawn of the place. "It's well guarded and well equipped. Some real money has been funneled into their hands. I saw enough rifles to outfit half the country."

"So if Ramirez is the source of the money, the rebels report to him now. He uses them to destabilize the country and undermine de la Reyes's government."

Coming to a realization, he straightened and looked at the other man. "We're not going to find Ramirez there, though. He's too smart to be caught with the rebels." He wasn't sure how he could use this information yet, but he'd file it away.

It was the sort of intel DHS or CIA might be interested in. So he'd make damn sure Ava never got close to it.

Just the thought of the woman left a burning sensation in his chest. He'd left her standing at Gonzalez's quarters earlier this evening without a word, too troubled by the thought that had occurred to him. Every moment he spent alone with her, even professionally, was dangerous on some level. It weakened his resolve. Made him soften toward her, and he couldn't afford even that small weakness.

His special ops background had left him with a black-and-white view of the world. And the number-one lesson he'd learned from his time in the military was that you didn't go into danger with people at your side you couldn't trust.

You damn sure didn't go to bed with them.

He hadn't taken Ava to bed, but he'd wanted to. And if he were honest, the thought lingered in the back of his brain at every second of every day. Memories of the moments spent pressed up against her in that damn take-me bed learning for himself the softness of her skin and the scent of her hair.

A soldier didn't lower his defenses when under attack, and his entire relationship with Samuelson had been just that. Ava was one more tool in the man's arsenal. Cael had to remember that, because she represented his best opportunity to destroy the man.

And, he thought grimly, he'd shed this conscience that seemed to be working overtime whenever he thought of using her. She'd displayed no such sensitivities about undermining him.

But as quickly as the thought occurred, he was forced to temper it. She'd come here all too willing to spy for Samuelson. But he was betting she'd been duped about the man's purposes. Hell, he knew from personal experience just how convincing the agent could be. His jaw tightened as he recalled just how far the man would go to get what he wanted.

He also knew how easily the facade would drop when he

was crossed. And Cael couldn't waste time worrying about the fallout for Ava once Samuelson realized she'd misled him, at Cael's direction. She deserved whatever twists came her way for going along with the man in the first place.

He told himself that. Tried to believe it.

"We can't do anything with the information right now," Reynolds was saying regretfully. It took a moment for Cael to follow the line of conversation back to the rebel camp. "We don't have the manpower. Could be close to two hundred in the camp…we'd need at least six guys."

Cael gave a quick grin of appreciation at the man's confidence. But it was close to the truth. He'd teamed with Reynolds in the military. The man had been at his side in more than one deadly situation. "That's not our mission here. At least not right now. When we get the whole team together… then we'll see where we're at on the investigation for de la Reyes. Who knows? Maybe he'll want to turn this information over to his military at some point."

Reynolds shrugged, but Cael could read the regret in his expression. "Camp probably won't be there much longer. You know as well as I do how mobile they are."

"We'll have to take that chance. Keeping de la Reyes safe is our priority. If we can find whoever is working for Ramirez, get to the man through them, the rebels will be no threat. Their enemy is whoever they are being paid to battle. And we may have gotten a valuable lead."

Carefully, he folded up the maps and the directions Reynolds had written to the camp. "Perez checked in earlier tonight. The Jeep driven by the men who fired on us on the way to the palace was reported stolen a week ago. Dental records have been matched on both of the victims. One is a brother of one of the air traffic controllers working at the airport the day our flight came in."

"We figured something like that," Reynolds commented.

"Perez is with the police right now for the interrogation."

And he doubted it was going easily on the controller. South American countries' police weren't bound by the same protocol American police were. The interview could get brutal, given what the man was suspected of.

Shrewdly, he studied the man who was as close to him as a brother. "Get some sleep. We can use some help covering the shifts on de la Reyes and Gonzalez."

"I wouldn't mind taking a shot at Gonzalez."

"Let's wait until we have the security cameras at the bank. Maybe we'll have something to hit him with later." Cael's cell phone rang, and he reached into his pocket to draw it out, read the number on the screen.

It was the information broker he'd called this morning. The one he'd charged with digging up Ava Carter's secrets.

"I have to get this. Have Sibbits show you where your room is." As Reynolds retreated, Cael answered the phone, anticipation swirling in his gut. Not even to himself would he admit that the thought of learning more about the woman was appealing in itself. She'd been maddenly closemouthed about anything remotely personal.

But fifteen minutes later Cael finished the conversation, a much different emotion careening inside him. It was, he thought bleakly, like getting an inadvertent peek at someone's dirty laundry. Except in this case not so inadvertent.

But he understood her now far better than he had ever thought he would. Understood why she hid her past. The impact the secrets could have on her career.

The only questions that remained were whether he could follow through and blackmail her with the information, in an attempt to gain her cooperation with Samuelson.

And whether he could live with himself if he did.

Because her shift came early the next morning, Ava turned in right after she'd eaten and showered. She came awake before dawn, fully alert.

Eyes getting used to the darkness, she saw what had awakened her. Each of them had been given a wrist communicator. It would vibrate and light up when there had been a breach in the security at the palace.

It was glowing and vibrating now.

Ava rolled out of bed and shrugged into her vest, fastening it with one hand as she grabbed her weapon with the other. Racing to the door of her room, she unlocked it and was speeding down the hall in less than ten seconds.

The perimeter of presidential guard was three deep inside the palace, she recalled, forgoing the elevator for the stairs. But it was impossible to tell from the wrist unit whether the inner or outer perimeter had been breached. And for some reason, the radio element didn't seem to be working.

On the main level she saw Reynolds, looking grim and dangerous with his Luger ready. Shouts sounded in the distance, and she could hear the rush of the presidential guardsmen.

"Inner or outer perimeter?" she called to Reynolds.

"Outer. Coming up through the front gate." He headed toward the front door, which already was crowded with guards.

The drive from the gate to the palace was at least a mile. When it got closer to the structure it swung in a wide semicircle. She let Reynolds cover the front and veered off to sprint toward the side entrance. If she could get to it in time, she could stop the driver before he ever made it to the palace entrance.

Elbowing her way through the guards, she had a moment to recognize they were holding their position, three deep inside each door, twelve feet apart, just as Cael had told them.

But then she was racing by them to the door, yelling to the closest guard closest in Spanish, "What's the visual?"

"Black limo, unidentified occupants."

"Open the door."

The door was unlocked and swung open as Ava hit it, taking the stairs at a leap and racing across the lawn. The lawn was soft as velvet beneath her bare feet. She could see the headlights first, spearing through the darkness. Recognized the shape of the vehicle slowly rolling up the drive before her.

She came to a sudden halt, raised her weapon. Took one deep breath and then fired two shots, one each into the front and back tire.

The limo came to a shuddering halt.

Ava was aware of the guards running up toward her, but it was to Reynolds she called, "Order a check of the undercarriage." The man snapped out an order in Spanish and several guards ran to fetch the equipment to carry out the search.

In a louder voice she shouted to the driver, *"Camine del coche con sus brazos levantados."*

But the driver and his passenger—she could see at least one in the backseat through the tinted windows—remained inside the car.

"Usted tiene treinta segundos para vaciar el coche antes de ques comencemos a tirar."

Ten seconds ticked by. Adrenaline spiked higher with each passing instant. Twenty seconds. Ava bit out an order to the nearby guards in Spanish. "Weapons loose." The surrounding guardsmen sighted their rifles.

Then slowly, the driver door inched open to frame a Hispanic man who looked to be in his mid-thirties, wearing a chauffeur's uniform in the same midnight black as the car.

"Don lanzamiento de t! Don lanzamiento de t!"

"Get out of the car with your hands in the air," Ava instructed in Spanish. When he did so, she gestured for two of the guards to search him, as a team of others, under Reynold's supervision, began inspecting the undercarriage of the vehicle for explosives.

She took position at the open door to point her rifle toward the lone occupant in the backseat. But before she could utter another order, the back passenger seat swung open and a petite whirlwind of fury exited, along with a spate of rapid-fire Spanish.

"How dare you! Who are you and what have you done with Tonio? I demand to be taken to him at once." The enraged woman slapped at a rifle barrel held by a nearby guard and spun to advance on Ava.

"If you have harmed my Tonio, I promise you will pay. I will kill you myself!"

Coolly, Ava stood her ground, not lowering her weapon even as the guard's voices sounded behind her.

"Marissa Mejido y Fuente. *Es el presidente novia de s.*"

The president's girlfriend? Ava exchanged a look with Reynolds, who also had turned at the words. His expression looked as blank as she felt. McCabe hadn't mentioned a girl-friend to contend with. For that matter neither had de la Reyes.

But the guards all seemed to recognize her.

Ava lowered her weapon. "Search the interior of the vehicle," she directed two of the men in Spanish. She switched her attention to the woman, continuing in the same tongue. "We are here to protect the president. He hasn't told us to expect you. He will be alerted of your presence here, but before you go inside I will have to search you."

Fuente's reaction was immediate and vitriolic. "You will not touch me! I demand to be taken at once to Tonio."

Ava engaged the safety and handed her rifle to a nearby guardsmen before approaching the woman. Fuente flexed her fingers and leaped at her. Ava jerked her head back, but felt the woman's nails rake down the side of her throat. Irritated, she grabbed Fuente's arm and yanked her off balance, using the woman's own weight against her as she took her down, keeping her there with one knee to her back.

With Fuente screeching, Ava swiftly and professionally frisked her for weapons. The short black cocktail dress had a plunging neckline and not much fabric to hide a weapon. Ava got up, took the woman by the arm and pulled her upright, giving her a little shake. "Behave yourself and we'll take you inside," she said grimly in Spanish. "Touch me again and I'll dump you in the fountain. Understand?"

"You will be sorry for this!" Fuente shook her hair back out of her extraordinarily beautiful face and balled her fists. "Tonio will see that you pay for your mistreatment of me!"

Ava felt the trickle of blood on her neck. Retrieving her weapon without relinquishing her grip on the woman's arm, she nudged her forward toward the side entrance of the palace. "*Your* mistreatment? And yet I'm the one bleeding. Go figure."

"This is an outrage, Tonio!" Marissa Mejido y Fuente paced the president's opulent personal living room and pointed her finger at a silent Ava, standing just inside the door. "That…that she-devil attacked me! She threatened me and pushed me down. Held a gun on me. I demand that she be imprisoned!"

"English, please, Marissa." De la Reyes crossed to hand her a glass of red wine, patting her hand. "Not all of our guests speak Spanish."

"Guests!"

Even Cael could feel the venom in the look she tossed at Ava, but she'd switched to English as requested, and sipped at the wine de la Reyes had supplied. "What is she doing here, dressed like a rifle-carrying *puta* and terrorizing your visitors?" Fuente shot him a distrustful look, as well. "What are any of them doing here? Why do you have so much security? You assured me the danger was over. Why are these foreigners here?"

But rather than answer her question, de la Reyes asked one of his own. "I didn't expect you back in the country for another two weeks. What of the modeling competition in Buenos Aires?"

The woman studied the man shrewdly before unexpectedly striding up to Cael and demanding, "Tell me what is going on. Tonio will try to hide things, or tell some but not all. You, I think, can give me the answers I seek."

Cael flicked a glance over at his operatives. Perez hadn't reported back yet, but besides Ava, Sibbits, Reynolds and Benton were all there. Next his gaze moved to de la Reyes, who gave him a little shrug.

"The president's would-be assassin in the States was killed before he could injure Antonio. The person who saved him, you might be interested to know, was Ava Carter." He nodded in her direction, noted that while the woman glanced at Ava, her focus was on the president.

"A lieutenant in the presidential guard was killed in the act," Cael continued. "Pedro Cabrerra. My company was hired by the president for added security in the States. When it became apparent that his presidential guard had been compromised, our contract was extended to accompany him back here until his safety has been secured. A second attempt was made on the president's life when he returned to San Baltes."

The woman gave a great shuddering breath before launching herself into de la Reyes's arms. The man managed, barely, to catch her wineglass before it drenched them both.

Cael looked away as the man held Marissa close, murmuring in her ear. He caught sight of Ava then and observed welts on her throat, red and raw with dried blood congealed on them. Relatively minor wounds. So it was ridiculous to feel this edge of worry for her.

Fuente's earlier description of her had been scathing, but Ava's appearance would have caught the attention of anyone new on the scene. At first glance it appeared as though she wasn't wearing anything beneath the armored vest, but he recognized the stretchy camisole and loose-fitting shorts below. She'd been wearing something similar the morning he'd accosted her in her bed.

He pushed that thought away before it could heat and distract him. But the scene Fuente had described was all too easy to visualize. He could picture a scantily clad armed Ava taking down the ultrafeminine model. And he didn't possess near enough determination to wipe *that* image from his mind.

Gently, de la Reyes set Marissa away from him, presenting her with a handkerchief taken from the pocket of his robe. He'd retired to his quarters with Benton on guard outside his door when the alarm had sounded. Cael had gone immediately to the president's side, handling communications from within the quarters.

"You still haven't answered my questions, Marissa," de la Reyes was saying. "Why are you back so soon? And why did you not call first before arriving so late this evening?"

The woman wiped daintily at her tear-streaked face. "My agent is quite displeased with me, but I insisted he cancel my appearance in Rio de Janiero. I've been so worried, I could not bear to be away from you any longer. I felt an urgency here." She touched a fist to her stomach as she gazed up at him. "I could think of nothing but seeing you as soon as possible."

"What I want to know is how she bypassed the security system on the gate," Cael said bluntly, his gaze drilling into the president. "We were led to believe you had retained the only remote access that would open the entrance."

A slight frown marring his brow, de la Reyes took a step away from Fuente. "I did. And Marissa has never been given a remote."

Her eyes flashing, she retorted, "No, Tonio has never offered one to me." And it was clear to everyone in the room that she smarted from the slight. "It was Captain Gonzalez who gave me the remote before I left the country last time. At least he recognized that a woman in love should not be kept waiting outside the gates like a servant, begging for entrance."

The room had gone deadly quiet. Cael felt his operatives' eyes on him, but his mind was racing furiously. Why would Gonzalez want an extra remote access to go to Fuente? How would that help him? If he wanted to double-cross the president, he was inside the grounds himself.

But security could be locked down by the president, he reminded himself grimly. And if de la Reyes had used the master security passkey, no one would get in or out of the palace grounds without a remote, the only one of which de la Reyes retained.

Until a spare had shown up in his girlfriend's possession.

Marissa was looking from one person to another, uneasiness in her expression. "Tonio, are you angry with me? I know I should have spoken to you about it first. I thought only to surprise you when I came back, not to cause this *alboroto*."

"I understand." De la Reyes was charming, if firm. "But your surprise entrance tonight caused a great deal of trouble for many people. I am happy to see you, of course. But I must ask that you give me the remote so we can be certain of our security."

"It is with my regular driver who brought me here," she said in a small voice. "You may retrieve it from him."

With a look, Cael directed Sibbits to do so. The operative crossed to the door and slipped through it.

"I will send my men to get your bags. Please wait for me upstairs."

Fuente nodded submissively at de la Reyes's suggestion, but Cael had the distinct impression that the fiery beauty would not stay subdued for long. She surprised him, however, when she stopped on the way out the door in front of Ava.

"I wish to apologize."

From Ava's expression, she appeared as shocked as the rest of the occupants in the room.

"I thought only of myself, my own outrage. But you saved my Tonio's life, and for that I owe you a debt of gratitude I can never repay."

Cael watched Ava accept the woman's hand. Before she continued to the door, Marissa gave her an arch look. "But as his *novia* I must suggest that perhaps you put on more clothes for this job, *si*? Perhaps a uniform—" she made a graceful gesture indicating throat to ankle "—that covers up far more. A jealous woman can be very dangerous."

Ava touched her throat. "I'll remember that."

After one long smoldering look toward de la Reyes, Marissa glided out the door. And when it closed behind her, de la Reyes let out a sigh. Reaching for the glass of wine she'd left behind, he took a sip, holding up a hand to Cael. "I know what you are thinking."

"You left some pretty major parts out of your story when we were planning your security," he said shortly. Diplomacy be damned. The man's lack of candor could have turned into a real security nightmare. "You certainly never mentioned Ms. Fuente."

"Because she was not part of the immediate picture here." The man's tone held an imperious edge. "I could not forsee she would be back so soon or I would have warned her to stay away, as I did with my family. And I assure you, I had no idea she had a remote to the gate."

Another thing Gonzalez had to answer for. Cael sent Reynolds a meaningful look and the man inclined his head. The man's quarters would be searched again. They'd thought the remotes were all accounted for. Which meant someone had had another copy made, the one that had ended up in Marissa Fuente's hands.

"What else do you need from me tonight?" the president asked him. And Cael knew he wasn't imagining the exhaustion in the man's expression. He kept a grueling schedule and tonight's events would have disturbed the first full night's rest he'd attempted since his return.

"I'll finish briefing the guards. What do you want done with Ms. Fuente's limo driver?"

De la Reyes was already moving toward the door. "His background was thoroughly checked when we arranged for him to drive Marissa. He may stay until she leaves."

Cael felt a clutch of impatience as the man left the room.

If nothing else, the woman's presence here was bound to be a nuisance. So far the president had willingly curtailed his outside activities to make it easier to check his security. Based on the taste they'd gotten of Fuente tonight, something told Cael she wasn't going to be content to hang around the palace day in and day out without entertainment.

He'd need to make de la Reyes see that the woman's presence here was an unnecessary risk, a distraction they couldn't afford. But until then, he had to lock down the security and debrief the unit that had, for the most part, done a decent job of protection this evening.

"Benton, you're back on shift outside de la Reyes's quarters. Everyone else, with me for the debriefing session with the National Guardsmen."

It promised to be a very long night.

Chapter 7

Ava's long strides ate up the hallway. It was all Cael could do to keep up with her. "I don't know why you're embarrassed. Those security tapes revealed that you and Reynolds showed exemplary decision making out there tonight."

"Embarrassed?" She whirled with a suddenness that took him by surprise. When she approached on him, her finger stabbed him in the chest. "You're damn straight I have nothing to be embarrassed about. What I am is *pissed*. I did my job like the professional I am. I didn't appreciate having my appearance on that tape treated like fodder for a bachelor party."

"What?" Stunned at her temper, he could only stare at her. But a sneaky sliver of guilt stabbed at him. Because yeah, the image of Ava's long legs racing across the expanse of lawn, the armored vest hiding most of her clothing beneath was…unforgettable. And the sight of her, bare limbs gleaming in the moonlight, dark hair mussed, wielding the assault rifle with a deadly certainty, was going to be the subject of some sweat-drenched dreams for some time to come.

But damned if he was going to admit that to her. "Everybody in that room is a professional. I can assure you, our only thought was to review our security procedure from the time the gate was breached."

She stared at him, fire lighting her eyes and shooting color to her cheeks. "If you didn't notice the reaction of the guardsmen in there for the briefing, you're dangerously unobservant. I spent all day today dealing with their response to me because I'm a woman. And finally, finally at the end of the day I earned a bit of respect. Now…" She made a rude sound. "I'm going to have to start all over again tomorrow and I'm giving you fair warning, the next one of them that touches me will be nursing broken bones."

"One of them touched you? Why didn't you report that? I'll make sure—"

"I don't need your help," she said, punctuating each word with a finger jab to his chest. To avoid injury, he reached up to capture her hand in one of his. "I need respect. I want that tape confiscated before every guardsman in the unit has a copy."

"I'll take care of it." He didn't particularly like the idea of that himself, although his mind shied away from examining the reason too closely.

She stared at him suspiciously, but something in his expression must have convinced her, because the tension in her muscles eased infinitismally. "Men are stupid."

He caught up with her as she turned and started walking rapidly down the hallway again toward her room. "Well…yeah."

An unwilling smile tugged at the corner of her mouth. "Present company not excluded."

Given that his reaction to the tape had been exactly as she'd described, that was hard to argue with, as well. "Conceded."

"Don't be so agreeable, McCabe. It's creepy."

He grinned, punchy with a combination of sleep deprivation and adrenaline crash. "What can I say? We're a primitive lot, conditioned to respond to certain, ah…shall I say stimuli?"

"I'll agree with the primitive part." Reaching her door, she seemed to remember something. "I should give you this." She shifted her weapon to her other arm, fighting to loosen her wrist communicator. "It vibrated and the alarm worked, but I wasn't able to use the radio."

Frowning, he took the device from her. "You couldn't hear the orders?"

"No. I wasn't sure why the limo had been allowed through without halting it, but I met up with Reynolds and he passed along the orders."

"The guards on outer perimeter made a tactical error assuming the limo held Fuente." The security breach still burned. "The vehicle should have been stopped far earlier. Those responsible will be released from duty. All in all, though, most of them did their job. The silver lining is, at least now we know where our weakness is and can regroup." He reached by her to push open the door she'd unlocked. "Mind if I check the base?"

Without waiting for permission, he strode across the room, his gaze unerringly going to the bedside table, which held the communicator radio base that regulated the channels on the unit. Propping her rifle against the wall, he knelt beside the base and began fiddling with the knobs. Moments later, he hissed out a breath in disgust.

"Damn thing isn't on the wrong channel, it isn't working at all."

"I believe I mentioned that."

Her tone was dry. And very close. Glancing up, he saw she'd come to stand next to him after shedding the armored tac vest. "Yeah, but they should have been checked and in working order prior to our dispersing them." He unplugged the base unit and placed the wrist communicator on top of it before rising. "I'll take this back to my room and switch it with another. Maybe it has a short in it."

His position when he stood placed him very close to her. Too close. She was caught between him and that wide expanse of bed, the mussed turquoise covers looking like ripples in tropical lagoon. And his pulse, as if on cue, began to drum. His thoughts to fragment.

After the last time he'd been in this room, it was all too easy to imagine lying on that bed with her beside him. Beneath him. He could still recall the feel of her, supple muscle and soft curves. Could still taste her, that unique flavor that fired his blood and wiped his mind clean of instinct and suspicion, leaving only passion in its place.

As if recognizing his thoughts, she took a step back. Was brought up short by the bed pressing behind her knees. "No." Her voice was firm. But in her expression he saw a reflection of the desire he was trying desperately to stem in himself. "We aren't going to make the same mistake twice."

"That's good to hear." His mind splintered into two dueling parts, logic and temptation, the latter fueled by a horned, sharp-tailed demon spurring him on to insanity. His hand reached out, as if devoid of conscious decision, and cupped her jaw.

Her hand came up as if to push it away. Lingered to stroke. "You don't trust me."

The skin beneath her ear was baby soft. When he brushed his fingertips over it she shuddered. "I can't."

"So why should I trust you?"

He replaced his hand with his lips, tracing that delicate jawline with a string of whisper soft kisses. "You shouldn't."

Her response was muffled by his mouth over hers. And the jolt at her taste was enough to ignite his system.

He ate at her hungrily, anxious to get his fill before one of them, both of them came to their senses. This wasn't smart. She was right about that. And he, who was used to quantifying every risk, assessing every danger, was deviating from hard-learned experience by ignoring that fact.

His arm snaked around her waist and he drew her closer. He'd taken plenty of chances in his lifetime, after he was assured he controlled the situation. But he wasn't so sure he could control his reaction to her.

Ava wound her arms around his neck and kissed him back with a reckless fervor that had his heart beating a heavy tattoo in his chest. And when her tongue swept into his mouth, bold and demanding, hunger lunged inside him.

Cael hooked a finger in one strap and dragged it over her shoulder until her breast was freed from the fabric, then cupped it in his hand. The nipple was taut, a testament to her desire, and he teased it with his fingers even as his free hand swept inside the elastic of her shorts to cup her butt.

The tantalizing twin pleasure of bare flesh had flames licking through his veins. She was sleek softness with the whisper of muscle beneath. And his mouth went to her breast in a primal quest for flesh.

The taste of her rollicked through his system. With a few swift moves he could have her naked, and under him, this time free to taste and stroke and touch freely. He was a man who assessed danger for a living, and he faced it now, of a sort that was more lethal than usual. This woman made him forget his convictions. To set aside the cool calculation that had been instrumental to his survival. She represented a danger of a different sort.

And was all the more tempting for it.

He became aware of her fingers between their bodies, trying to undo the straps securing the vest he still wore. Rather than moving to help her, he squeezed the fullness of her bottom, his fingers grazing the cleft. He sucked from her nipple urgently, dimly aware that he was approaching the point of no return. Ready, damn ready, to dive over the edge and think about the consequences later.

She was only a few inches shorter than him, and he could still intimately recall from the time he'd spent on top of her how well they'd fit, every inch, every angle and hollow. Skin heating against skin.

The alarm shrilling in his mind barely registered. But her stillness did. With savage reluctance he raised his head and only then did he become aware that the sound was all too real. But rather than a mental alarm, it was a cell phone.

Hers.

Blinking to regain focus, he saw the cell on her bedside table. The international one he'd provided her with, along with every other member of the team, when she'd gotten on the plane. The screen was lit up now, as it gave one last burst of sound before falling silent.

It took another moment for understanding to filter through the fog of passion. He recognized the number showing on the screen before it went dark. Had seen it on his own cell screen a few times.

He released her with a suddenness that sent a chorus of protests from parts of his body that shouldn't get a vote. And comprehension rushed in, nearly rocking him off his feet with the enormousness of his miscalculation.

Ava still looked dazed. And when she reached for him again, God help him, it was all he could do to take a step back and scramble for the logic that had deserted him like a paratrooper from a flaming chopper.

"Better call him back," he said tersely.

His words must have registered, even if his tone didn't. She picked up the phone, fumbling with it as if she wasn't in total control of her muscles yet, and the evidence of her response nearly had him throwing back his head and howling his frustration.

Tension, of a far different sort than that of a few moments ago, shot his muscles with steel.

"I don't recognize—"

"I do." His jaw was clenched so tightly it ached. "It's Samuelson's."

She dropped the phone then with a clatter, but he knew he wasn't imagining the guilt flickering over her expression. "So does he have you reporting in on a regular schedule? If you missed a time, I wouldn't keep him waiting. He isn't known for his patience."

Ava straightened her clothing, then took several strides away from the bed. And farther from him. "I left him a message with my number when I got here. I haven't spoken to him since."

Cael didn't bother to sift through her words for truth and fabrication. His stupidity drumrolled in his head, hammered home just how colossal an error he'd almost made.

The irony was she'd warned him of just that before he'd reached for her.

The fury pumped through him in waves. He knew from experience what happened when you wanted something, someone too much. That depth of feeling inevitably blinded him to the truth, made him reach decisions based on emotion rather than logic.

It had him risking more than he should. And later, when reality slashed through longing, it made the crash brutally resounding.

"Maybe it's best you wait to call him later," he agreed. "I haven't ironed out all the details, but you can start feeding them to Samuelson each time you report in."

He noticed the rise of her chest. The effort it took for her to compose her features and face him with a dispassion to match his own. "I already told you I won't be part of that."

"I think you will." He cocked a derisive brow, saw her flush with the first tinge of annoyance. "My information broker is at least as thorough as the government databases."

She went still then, and the color that had so quickly flared to her cheeks leeched just as swiftly.

"It's always a crapshoot to figure the lengths people will go to hide something from their past, but I'm figuring you'd go pretty far to make sure no one knows Calvin Julson is your father."

If he hadn't reined his conscience in with a vicious grip, her expression might have caused him to soften. To take a step toward her and stroke away the flash of pain on her face.

But the last few minutes had taught him the danger of softening toward her. Of ignoring reality in favor of dreams.

She walked a few feet to grasp one of the four posters to the bed frame, as if in need of its support. Her tension was evident in her deathly pale face, in the white-knuckle grip she had on the frame.

"I figure Samuelson discovered that, too, and used it to force you to accept this assignment." He was willing to grant her that much. Ava would have needed powerful incentive to change her mind to join his team temporarily. The money might have been part. But not all.

She remained motionless. "He intimated. I thought he must know. But he didn't come out and say it."

Of course the man wouldn't. Cael reeled in his temper, forced himself to think clearly. The agent would reveal only enough to get what he wanted. He was a master at playing people, using their vulnerabilities against them in a manner guaranteed to have them falling in line with whatever he asked of them.

Cael had been suckered himself, once upon a time.

Steeling himself against the sight of her, shocked and dismayed, he said, "Well, I don't blame you for not wanting anyone to know of your relationship to Julson." And watched her, hawklike, for her reaction.

She swallowed. Seemed to search for words. "I haven't spoken to my father in over fifteen years. He isn't part of my life. And I can hardly be held accountable for genetics, can I? It's not like I had a choice in my parentage."

Her last statement struck a chord, but he refused to let it alter him from his course. "Good line. I wonder how your

SWAT commander would feel about it. Or your captain. I think we both know what the press would do if they were fed the information. Local legendary SWAT sniper and detective affiliated with the most infamous white supremacist in the country? Every arrest you've ever made will be suspect. Every target you've ever taken out will have family pouring out of the woodwork. The city will be buried in discrimination lawsuits for decades."

Her deer-in-the-headlights expression gave him pause. He half expected her to toss his veiled threats back in his face. To invite him to do his worst. And he wondered, still, when push came to shove, if he'd be able to follow through.

But she did neither. She just looked at him with those dark and haunted eyes. And her words were like a knife twisting deep inside him. "Explain again how I'm supposed to tell you and Samuelson apart. Your tactics are the same. You go after a person's emotional jugular and hold a knife to it. And you…you're threatening to shred everything I hold dear. To destroy my life to get what you want. I used to think you two were carbon copies. But now I think you're worse than he is."

With every word she uttered his throat tightened until it threatened to strangle him. If she'd wielded a machete on him, she couldn't have wounded him more deeply.

He had to force himself to move. To round the corner of the bed where she still clung for support, and stride to the doorway. "The choice is yours. You cooperate with me and your secret is safe. But if you refuse…" He halted at the door, his hand on the doorknob, and looked over his shoulder back at her. "…then I'll destroy you along with Samuelson."

The rap at his door was unwelcome. Cael was on his balcony nursing a neat whiskey and battered scruples. He considered, for the space of a second, not answering it. Professionalism won out over surliness, and he shoved away from the railing, carrying his drink with him to the bedroom door.

He exchanged the glass for his weapon before he opened it. Found Reynolds standing on the other side.

The man didn't bat an eye at the gun. "Saw your light. Figured if you were still up you must have…" Obviously spying the drink setting on the dresser, he amended, "…and you do have liquor. What is it? Whiskey? Got another glass?"

Swinging the door open, Cael allowed the man to enter. He went to the bathroom and returned with a water glass. Pouring two fingers into it, he said, "I'm out of ice."

Reynolds reached for the glass. "Have you ever known me to be choosy?" Without another word he headed out onto the balcony Cael had deserted. Retrieving his drink, Cael followed him.

"Couldn't sleep," the man told him laconically, propping a hip against the balcony.

Cael nodded his understanding. Adrenaline did odd things to a person's body. Sharpened nerve endings to such a keen edge that rest was impossible until the effect was worn off. And Reynolds was an adrenaline junkie. So he'd pursued the type of life he was best suited for, as Cael had himself.

The two men were silent for a while as they sipped their drinks and stared out in the darkness. They knew each other well enough for the quiet to be companionable. They'd had each other's back more times than Cael wanted to remember. He couldn't think of anyone he trusted as implicitly.

"Could have been worse tonight," the other man mused. "Major screwup not stopping Fuente's limo sooner, but the inner perimeter held and the interior security looked solid. What'd you decide on the outer perimeter?"

"They've been terminated."

Reynolds nodded. There was no other choice. The men had proven that their judgment was flawed. That given a split-second decision, they made the wrong one. Whether a stupid mistake or a more calculated one, they needed to be weeded out before they made another error in judgment that could prove costlier.

"Carter was solid."

A knot fisted in the pit of Cael's belly. "Looked like it."

"Good nerves. Sharp decision making." Reynolds paused a moment to drink. "Took both tires out with one shot each, no night-vision goggles. Not too shabby."

"I saw the tape," Cael said shortly. His gut was starting to burn now. It suited him to blame the whiskey.

The other man grinned, a flash of white teeth in the near darkness. "Wouldn't mind seeing it again. Hell, wouldn't mind having that tape in my private collection. I got a thing for dangerous women. It's a sickness. And then that wrestling match with Fuente." He gave a suggestive whistle. "Worth the price of—"

"She's working for Samuelson."

The abrupt words successfully stemmed the rest of that sentence. Wiped the humor from Reynold's face with a swiftness that would have been comical under any other circumstances.

"How long have you known?"

"Long enough."

Cael felt Reynolds stare at him searchingly as he took another drink, welcoming the scorch of the whiskey down his throat.

"Do we have to watch for sabotage?"

We. The word had appreciation flickering. Cael looked at the man, closer to him than any brother could be. "No, she's solid for this assignment. He fed her a bogus line about wanting information on the government here to get her to agree to come. I figure he'll reveal his true purpose when she gets back to the States."

"He'll pump her for every fact observed about you and your handling of this mission, then twist that to suit his own purposes. Rat bastard."

It was no coincidence that their minds ran along such similar paths. "If he wants to manufacture a crap storm, the political climate is well suited for a reputation assassination, don't you think?" The performance of the private security contractors in Iraq had Congress looking at similar firms with a magnifying glass. And high-risk missions such as these were rife with opportunity for something to go wrong. It wouldn't take much spin from a man in Samuelson's position to lay the blame for any bloodshed squarely at Cael's doorstep. A congressional inquiry could tie him up for months. Close his business down. Ruin Cael's career.

"Well, if he just wants you destroyed instead of dead he's modified his objective. Any chance that's Carter's true purpose here?"

"She's a sniper, not an assassin."

Reynolds took a long drink. "Person's occupation can change given enough motivation. The way Samuelson works, he'd have provided her with some decent motivation."

"You could say that." Cael stared broodingly into the night, swirling the amber liquor around in his glass. "I imagine he's discovered the same thing I did. She's Calvin Julson's daughter."

The liquor in Reynolds's glass sloshed precariously as he jerked toward Cael. "No shit? How deep was that buried?"

"I doubt it was something she put on her job application," he said drily. Julson was, in his estimation, emotionally unbalanced. He'd seen TV clips of the man, lean and tough as shoe leather, spouting the sort of hateful vitriol that incited violence against whichever minority he was railing against at the time. He'd narrowly managed to avoid a conspiracy conviction two years ago for the murder of a homosexual couple living in Montana.

It still astounded him that the man's blood ran through Ava's veins. Little wonder she'd disavowed him.

"We can use this," Reynolds said surely. He was deep in strategy mode now. "Samuelson doesn't know it, but he's handed us a weapon in Carter. You're already figuring on using her, right?" He didn't wait for an agreement. Their minds worked similarly most of the time. "Carter doesn't want this out, she'll have no choice but to agree. We manufacture a carefully edited story about circumstances down here that put you in a less than stellar light of course."

"Of course."

"Samuelson takes the bait, mounts a full-fledged inquiry, leading the charge, discovers too late that he's been had and ends up with his reputation in shambles." Reynolds cocked a brow at him. "Is that what you're thinking?"

Useless to deny it. "Something along those lines."

"But here's the death blow for that prick." Propping his forearms on the railing, Reynolds drained his glass. "We can still kill his entire career just by letting this spin out. Getting proof of him working with Carter. Then we leak who she really is, and any credibility he has is shot. This is a win-win for us." He raised his empty glass with a grin. "Congratulations, buddy. We've finally been handed a way to give that son of a bitch a figurative bullet between the eyes."

"Destroying Carter in the process."

His tone apparently wasn't quite as even as he'd strived for. Reynolds's look sharpened. "Well, yeah. But she's collateral damage, right? You can't afford to worry about her when an opportunity like this falls into your lap. You take it and do what you have to."

"Right."

"It'll be a pleasure helping you plan just how to paint that pock-faced bastard into a corner and finish him off." Reynolds clapped him on the shoulder before setting the empty glass down and cheerfully saying good-night.

Moodily, Cael finished off his drink as the door closed in back of the man. There was nothing Reynolds liked better than plotting strategy. He'd have two or three lines of action to suggest in a matter of hours. Given their affinity for this sort of thing, Cael would be very much surprised if whatever his friend came up with didn't match pretty closely the tentative strategy he'd mapped out.

She's collateral damage, right?

No matter how he tried, he couldn't get Reynolds's words out of his head. They shouldn't burn and char a hole through his system. It would be a mistake to forget Ava had signed on for this. To spy, if nothing else, reporting details back to Samuelson that would be twisted to hang Cael.

Okay, maybe she had no way of knowing what the man was. What he'd use her for. But she was a cop. A sniper. She knew few missions went as planned. How easily they went awry and how quickly something black and white could be painted with shades of gray. She assumed that risk every day on the job.

Toying with the empty glass, he shifted his attention to Samuelson. There was little he wouldn't do to bring the man down. He'd been a malevolent force in Cael's life since they'd met. The agent had done his best to destroy him. Certainly he'd destroyed his mother. So there was little he wouldn't do to return the favor. Even if it meant using Ava Carter.

But his conscience was like a noose, strangling him from the inside. He'd have to find a way to set it aside. He couldn't afford to be soft now, when everything he'd worked for was being handed to him on a platter.

He couldn't afford to let concern for Ava sway him from the most important act of his life.

Ava sat on the bed, propped on the pool of pillows staring into the shadows. Sleep was out of the question.

It seemed obvious that it had only been a matter of time until her past became known. Odd how that thought seemed so clear now, when she would have violently disagreed with it weeks earlier. Certainly she'd never taken particular efforts to conceal it. She'd been seventeen when she stopped trying to contact her father. Stopped begging him to allow her back into his life. She was too numb to experience the familiar twist of shame at the memory. And then she'd met Sammy, married him and moved to California. Kept his name after they divorce, and even that had had as much to do with her and Alex sharing the same last name as with hiding her relationship with Calvin Julson.

Shoulders slumped, she turned her thoughts to damage control. Because she was through being manipulated. First by Samuelson and now by Cael. The past could only be used to hurt her if she wanted it kept hidden. Remove the secret, remove the power of using it as a weapon.

But the thought of what she had to do made her stomach tangle in greasy knots. She'd lied to Alex all his life. Ironic that she'd been scrupulously honest about the boy who'd gotten her pregnant. She had every intention of going through with her promise to her son that she'd allow him to contact the man if he wanted to when he was eighteen.

But she'd told him since he could ask that he had no grandparents, other than Sammy's father. No cousins. No living relatives on her side at all. She'd been protecting him by shielding him from the truth. It wasn't easy confronting who and what her father was.

But she'd been protecting herself as well. Because she hated, *hated* considering what she'd been on her way to becoming before her father had kicked her out.

The hours ticked by as she wrestled with the rationalizations and the sick fear that her son would detest her for the lie. Despise her for the truth. But as dawn tinged the sky outside the window, she knew exactly what she had to do.

Reaching for the phone, she dialed Alex's cell number.

Chapter 8

Ava exchanged a look with Sibbits and Benton as they walked into the conference room. If all of McCabe's operatives were in one place, who was guarding de la Reyes and Gonzalez?

All of them took chairs at the table. And it occurred to her, surveying Cael's grim expression, that the last forty-eight hours hadn't been kind to him. She refused to spare him any sympathy. She hadn't spoken to him alone since the scene in her room. When he'd had her in his arms one moment, threatened her the next. Nor was she looking forward to their next conversation. But for now, she focused on what he had to tell them. It was obvious from his expression that it was urgent.

"You know that Perez never returned from the police interrogation of the airline dispatcher."

Ava and the other two operatives nodded at McCabe's terse words. She knew Cael had gotten more and more concerned, especially after talking to the police captain. Perez had left headquarters after spending nearly twelve hours on the interrogation. The police claimed they hadn't seen him since.

"How do we know we can trust the policia in this country?" offered Sibbits. His rubbed his hand over his graying crew cut. "Everyone else is suspect. Why not them?"

"The interrogation did convince them that the dispatcher was in Ramirez's employ. And they may or may not be corrupt. Or others working for Ramirez could have been watching. We have to consider that Perez might have been followed and scooped up by them after leaving the police headquarters."

The mood in the room turned grim. "The hospitals have been checked?" Ava asked.

Cael nodded. "He's not in jail, he's not in a hospital. He's not in the morgue."

She wondered if she imagined the bleak unspoken "yet" at the end of that statement.

"I sent Reynolds out to sniff around last night. See if he could shake some information loose from any of the informants he's worked with. He hasn't reported in."

Uneasiness filled her. Protocol dictated reports at least every eight hours. Reynolds appeared to be a consummate professional. If anyone could find Perez, it'd be him, or Cael himself.

But his being out of communication for so long was extremely worrying.

"What this means to us is we're down two men for the time being. I've got two guardsman on Gonzalez right now. God knows they can't get him out of his quarters without blowing themselves to hell and back. And de la Reyes is in the next room having breakfast with Fuente. It's going to take the four of us to rotate between shifts. But being shorthanded is dangerous, too. I want each of you to give me names of guardsmen that have impressed you. Ones you trust more than the others. We're going to have to start giving a few of them more responsibility, at least where they can be supervised."

"Where are we on their bank account audits?"

Cael reached for a mug of coffee sitting in front him, took a drink. "No other unexplained sums of money showed up in any guardsmen's accounts. Of course they wouldn't have had to deposit a bribe, either. But there was a large deposit made to the airport dispatcher. Hopefully this means we can afford to trust the presidential guard more in the coming days."

"What have you learned about the remotes?"

There was a lethal edge to Cael's tone. "I'll be talking to Gonzalez again in a few minutes. Reynolds and I spent the last thirty-six hours interviewing the National Guardsmen. More questions about him have arisen." He glanced at his watch. "That's it. Sibbits and Benton, get some sleep. Carter, you're on de la Reyes. I'll take Gonzalez. We'll have another briefing this evening."

Ava slid her chair back and rose, turning toward the door. Cael's voice stopped her. "Carter, I'd like to speak to you for a minute."

She was tempted, sorely tempted, to continue out the door. She'd managed to evade being alone with him for two days. It hadn't been easy to tamp down the trepidation and antagonism their last scene together had fostered. Even now, her chest was going tight and nerves were clutching in her belly.

The reaction annoyed her. Cael McCabe wasn't going to be given this kind of power over her. Not anymore. Not on any level.

She forced herself to meet his gaze, hoping none of the welter of emotion showed in her expression. When the door clicked quietly behind her, leaving the room empty except for the two of them, she could feel the walls shrinking in, crowding her.

Cael was silent for a moment. But his gaze, fixed on hers, was searching. She wasn't going to remember what had happened the last time they were alone together. That path led to betrayal. Instead she'd recall what he'd said after he'd released her.

A man ready to take her to bed one minute and issuing threats the next exuded a kind of danger that owed nothing to the physical. And a woman who was still attracted in the face of his ruthlessness was nothing short of stupid. He wouldn't be allowed to slip under her guard again.

But that vow felt hollow alongside the sliver of concern that pierced her as the silence strung out between them. He looked like the last two days had been long on worry and short on sleep. Certainly the disappearance of Perez would be weighing on him.

Unwilling to break the taut silence, she waited for him to speak. When he did, his words helped stiffen her will even as they flayed her feelings.

"I'm hoping that the last couple days have given you an opportunity to reevaluate your position."

Deliberately misunderstanding, she said, "You mean professionally? Because I have to admit, dealing with Marissa Fuentes's theatrics every day does test my patience. If she orders me to fetch something for her one more time I may have to place her in a choke hold."

As a diversionary tactic, it failed miserably. The look in his pale green eyes remained intent. "I don't want this thing to end up hurting you. Whatever else happens, I don't want you being…" A muscle jumped in his jaw. "…collateral damage."

"Perfect. We're agreed, then."

She turned toward the door and he was at her side before she could reach for the handle. With a hand on her elbow, he spun her around to face him again.

"Dammit, Ava, be reasonable." His face was shoved too close to hers for comfort. His voice terse. "Do you honestly think you can walk away from this? It's easy to say you're washing your hands of the whole thing, but Samuelson will never allow that. He's a dangerous son of a bitch and vindictive as hell. He'll destroy you."

She ignored the quick shudder down her spine. "Or you will?"

He let go of her suddenly. Took a few steps away as if by establishing a physical distance he could achieve an emotional one as well. "I've been all around this thing for the last forty-eight hours. There's no way out for you. If you tell Samuelson you won't cooperate, first he'll persuade, then he'll threaten. Don't kid yourself about him. His standing gives him a certain amount of power and he uses that to get what he wants, damn anyone in his way."

"I have only your word that what he wants isn't exactly what he presented to me—a report on the government's stability here."

He gave a humorless smile. "Did it ever occur to you to wonder what brought DHS to Metro City?"

She had, in fact, wondered that very thing in Sanders's office. "The assassination attempt," she said, with more certainty than she felt. "The terrorism being sponsored by Ramirez and his men."

"There is no terrorism in San Baltes that endangers the U.S." Cael made a short dismissive gesture with his hand. "That was all bogus to explain Samuelson's interest here. It was my involvement with de la Reyes that had him following us from D.C. to California. Me being on the same continent as the man is powerful temptation. The assassination attempt must have given him the idea to use this contract against me." His smile was bleak. "It wouldn't be the first time."

That the two had a history had been apparent from the beginning. But Ava didn't ask the questions that were trembling on her lips. Because reasons didn't matter. "Neither of you is going to be allowed to use me. And both of you are going to have to deal with that."

She suspected he was grinding his teeth. "You are dangerously naive," he muttered. "You can't play a human Switzerland here. You won't be allowed to remain neutral. Everything

I threatened you with, you can be damn sure he's already thought of. Planned for. And he won't hesitate to follow through if you refuse him."

"But you would?"

Something flickered across his expression, there and gone too quickly to be identified. He looked away. "The only way out for you is to help me. By the time he realizes the part you played in his downfall, he'll be defanged. He won't have the power to hurt you or to plot revenge. He'll be too damn busy trying to keep his ass out of a federal court for misuse of his position."

It shouldn't have hurt, to listen to him reach for any tool to elicit her assistance. She'd already learned the lengths he'd go to get it.

But it did hurt. Intensely. "I can't tell you how much I appreciate your concern for me." She made no effort to keep the sarcasm from her tone. "But I'll take my chances."

"Don't be stupid." Cael slammed the palm of his hand on the conference table, making her jump. "I can't protect you from him, don't you get that? I've been all over this thing and I can't figure a way to keep you out of it, even if I wanted to. You either let him use you to destroy me or you help me bring him down. There is no third option. The man is treacherous."

She squelched the warmth that threatened to bloom. His supposed worry for her was a sham. Nothing about the man could be trusted as genuine. Except for his hatred of Samuelson.

There was an unfamiliar tightness in her throat. "Did the thought ever occur that you might have misjudged the man? That your hatred for him has blinded you to who and what he is?"

The stillness that came over him was lethal. His fist clenched at his side so tightly that the knuckles turned white. She had a moment to wonder at his reaction before his next words, uttered in a flat, bleak tone, scattered any formal thought.

"I know exactly who and what is he. Better than most people could. He's my father."

* * *

Cael's mood was dangerous as he strode up to Gonzalez's quarters. With a terse jerk of his head, he indicated for the guardsman on duty to step aside before turning to the security device on the door. Using his body to shield his actions from any interested eyes, he tapped in the code and drew his weapon. It would be careless to let his temper affect the upcoming interview. Unprofessional to allow the scene with Ava to color his judgment.

The woman had been allowed too much control over him already.

What other reason could there be for him blurting out the truth about his relationship with Samuelson? He'd done his damnedest to forget it over the years. What other reason could explain the direction of his strategizing for the last couple of days? Every plan he and Reynolds had plotted out for bringing down Samuelson had all had the same flaw. They all meant Ava would be ruined in the process.

Even if he didn't use her in the man's demise, she'd get caught up in the fallout. That was unavoidable. And why the hell, he wondered bitterly, gesturing for the guardsman to leave his weapon at the door, should he care about that? Now, when Samuelson's destruction was within reach, why would he start worrying about a woman he hadn't even known two weeks ago?

It couldn't be allowed, he thought grimly, opening the door to allow the guardsmen to precede him. He stepped inside the quarters, weapon ready, and surveyed Gonzalez's familiar contemptuous expression. He couldn't afford to be weak when he could imagine what Samuelson was planning. He was through playing defense with the man.

And he was through—he'd have to be through—worrying about Ava Carter.

"You will interpret for us," he told the guardsman tersely. The man, Eduardo Vasquez, looked uneasy. But when Cael gestured for him to pull up two chairs the man did so, sinking slowly into one with a nod from him.

Remaining standing, Cael surveyed Gonzalez. The man stared back unrepentantly. He made a short remark that had Vasquez fidgeting, sliding a glance toward Cael but not quite meeting his eyes.

"The captain…he say that you are…uh…"

"I'm aware of his opinion of me," Cael said drily. He lowered his weapon but didn't reholster it. "Believe me, it's reciprocated."

Vasquez screwed up his brow, but Cael didn't bother to explain further. Instead he took the free chair and turned it around so he could sit on it backward, resting his arms on its back.

"You are a liar," he said clearly to Gonzalez. "And now we have proof of that." He waited for Vasquez to haltingly interpret before reaching in his shirt and withdrawing a stack of photos. He handed them to the guardsman, who looked through them, clearly puzzled.

"Give them to the captain," Cael directed, watching carefully as the younger man approached Gonzalez. But he did as directed, dropping the batch of pictures in the man's lap before returning to take his seat again.

"I assume you will recognize the man in the picture."

Gonzalez stared at him a moment longer, insolence etched in his expression.

"You ought to, anyway. He's your nephew."

When Vasquez translated, Gonzalez's eyes widened. He picked up the pictures awkwardly with his bound hands and looked down at the top one. Any doubt Cael might have had was erased when he saw recognition and shock flare in the man's expression.

"The date and time he was caught on camera at your bank coincides with when the deposit was made into your account. You remember. The deposit you don't know anything about?"

Cael's tone was caustic. Vasquez spoke in rapid Spanish, his earlier unease seemingly dissipated in the face of the news.

"The chief…he say his nephew would not do such a thing. There must be another…how do you say it…explanation."

"I have a real good idea what that might entail," Cael put in grimly. "We've got unexplained cash appearing in Gonzalez's account and his nephew at the scene at the same time. Couple that with the fact that his nephew seems to have disappeared, and I'd have to be an idiot to believe his protests of innocence." He grinned sharkishly. "I'm not an idiot."

After a swift give-and-take in Spanish, Vasquez reported, "The chief cannot explain that. He worries about his nephew. That perhaps he was made to do something and now a bad thing has happened to him."

"You know what worries me? That maybe his nephew is working for Ramirez. That Gonzalez is, too. And that he's still lying about it, hoping to avoid a firing squad for his betrayal of his president."

Vasquez was silent for a moment. His expression, when he turned back to the captain, was forbidding as he translated.

"You are wrong about him. He say he would protect the president with his life."

"Sure." Cael nodded, tapping the side of his Luger with his index finger. He watched Gonzalez's eyes track the movement nervously. "That probably explains his giving an extra remote to Fuente and keeping its existence from the president. Who else has he given a remote to? How many copies has he made?"

Vasquez translated in a rapid spate of Spanish and Gonzalez shook his head vehemently as he answered. His protest was cut short when the younger man heatedly responded again, his retort effectively silencing the chief.

"He denies that he ever gave Marissa Fuente a remote. Or that he made any extra copies of them. I told him what I told you. That I saw him give it to her one day in the palace. That I had left something in the hall and had come back for it."

Vasquez's tone was bitter. "He lies now. Because I saw that with my own eyes. It is hard not to think he lies about everything."

Gonzalez looked from one of them to another, his expression growing panicked. He spoke pleadingly, his earlier bravado vanished.

"He admit it now. That Miss Fuente pleaded so prettily for a remote and he only agreed because he thought the president knew. She promised him so."

"Hard to know what to believe," Cael said in a hard tone, staring at the man with antipathy rising. There was little as despicable as a man who sold out his own to line his pockets. "Should I believe him a traitor or merely an incompetent fool? What would he believe, if all this evidence was gathered and implicated one of his men?"

When Vasquez translated, Gonzalez remained stubbornly silent.

Cael fought to rein in his frustration. "Ask him what he was plotting. Did Ramirez plan for the next assassin to use Fuente and her remote to get him inside the palace walls? Or was he going to send a little present along in the trunk of her limo sometime? Given the bullshit security Gonzalez was providing, it wouldn't have been too difficult for Ramirez to pack an explosive in a car that would be given access to the palace's inner perimeter."

The chief shook his head violently as Vasquez translated. A moment later the guardsman reported, "He say he was guilty of an error in judgment but not of betraying the president. He would protect the president with his life."

The chair clattered to the floor as Cael lunged from it. Closed the remaining distance to the captain and pressed his weapon against the man's temple. "You put de la Reyes's life at risk." He struggled to rein in the temper surging. "By doing so you put your country's stability at risk. You're either a miserable excuse for a security professional or you're collaborating with a scumbag drug dealer. Which is it?"

Gonzalez went very still, his eyes squeezing shut. And for a moment, for one dangerous second, it wasn't the captain of the presidential guard sitting there, waiting for death. It was Dennis Allen Samuelson. A lifetime of resentment became a cauldron of frothing emotion. He hauled in a breath, fought for control.

And slowly, slowly tipped the barrel of the gun up. Stepped back. When he was sure he had his restraint on a leash, he spoke again. "The satisfaction of your death belongs to your president, not to me. It's him you'll answer to. Him and your country."

It was with great care that he left the quarters. Locked the door behind them. Reset the security system. His actions were automatic. They didn't require thinking. Right now, Cael desperately didn't want to think.

Because he didn't lose control. Not ever. And it was staggering to consider just how close he'd come in there to doing just that.

"I thought Chief Gonzalez was a great man."

He started a little. He'd half forgotten that Vasquez was still there. The younger officer's gaze lit on his face for a moment. Slid by him.

"He hired me for this position. Impressed on me how important it was. My duty to protect the president. I thought he was a hero."

Vasquez headed in the direction of the guards' barracks, a dejected slump to his shoulders. And Cael knew the officer had learned a valuable lesson that day. He'd never have a case of hero worship again. No one would ever be regarded without a tinge of cynicism.

His disillusionment might strengthen him in the long run. Maybe then he wouldn't disappoint himself the way Cael just had earlier.

With his free hand, he rubbed at the knot of muscles bunched in his neck. Perspective was deserting him, at the worst possible time. The absence of Reynolds and Perez left them more shorthanded than they'd already been. They still had several more days before the other expected operatives would be joining them.

And Ava just might be right after all. Maybe he was allowing his hatred of Samuelson to blind him. In more ways than one.

Or maybe it was his growing obsession with her that was blinding him. Settling in for a long stint, he leaned a shoulder against the exterior wall of the house. He needed to clear his mind. Think like a soldier instead of a hormone-ridden teenager. He had Samuelson in his sights. He couldn't afford to be distracted with worries about fallout for her. On a mission, nothing could detour him from his target.

He had to remember that. And he needed to regain his famed dispassion, quickly. Before this whole thing went to hell around them because he was wasting time focusing on her.

"Ms. Carter."

The imperious tone grated Ava's nerve endings. She slid her gaze to Marissa Fuentes, who was gliding up to her wearing a gown more suited for life in a brothel than a quiet day at home.

"I am quite parched. You will bring me flavored water."

Ava read the gleam in the woman's eyes. She knew damn well Ava wasn't going to do her bidding. The same way she hadn't obeyed any of the last hundred commands the woman had made since she arrived. She issued them for one reason only. To get on Ava's nerves.

Since she'd learned it was the surest way to return the favor, she looked away and assumed a bland expression. The woman was bored here. Ava had known she would be. De la Reyes had resumed his schedule of meetings and teleconferences during the day, leaving Fuente at loose ends.

Of course, she amended silently, the woman rarely rose before noon so she didn't have all that much time to fill. It was unfortunate for Ava that she'd decided baiting the only female operative on the security detail was her favorite pastime.

Fuente snapped her fingers, dangerously close to Ava's nose. "Did you hear me? I want it now." When Ava still didn't answer, the woman smirked and turned to the guard nearest her. In Spanish she said, "Perhaps she is deaf as well as dumb. She will not be of much use to my Tonio if that is so."

From the corner of her eye Ava saw the guard start to smile before he caught her looking at him. He quickly sobered, saying nothing. And there was no ripple of reaction from the other guardsmen, either. Something had changed since she'd chewed them out the other day. She could at least be thankful for that.

Tiring of the game, the woman changed tactics. Surveying Ava critically from head to toe, she said, "How does a woman such as you hope to interest any male dressed as you are? You look like a man, I think, with clothes that hide any curves you might have." She paused, but Ava remained quiet. Her expression grew sly. "Or maybe you are a woman who is not a woman. Maybe it is not a man you are wanting to attract, *si?*"

Temper spiked through Ava's system. Leaning forward, she murmured, "You want to know what kind of woman I am? I'm the kind of woman who's going to kick your ass if you don't get out of here and let me do my job."

Fuente quickly took a step back before catching herself. Smoothing a hand down her gown, she tossed her hair. "I will speak to Tonio about your attitude. You are nothing but the help and you would do well to remember that." With that she swept away and out the door. De la Reyes, on the other side of the room on the phone, didn't seem to notice.

But some of Fuente's words had left a mark. Because Ava was increasingly wondering what kind of woman she was, too. She'd never been one to make excuses for a man's behavior. Had no patience for women who did. She'd learned at fifteen how to cut her losses and move on. Her boyfriend's profession of eternal love had died a quick and brutal death when she'd told him she was pregnant. She damn well hadn't hung around begging for more.

So it was pretty hard to understand the chemistry that, God help her, still flared to life whenever she and McCabe were in the same room. He'd threatened her. Tricked her. Stated his intention to blackmail her. She ought to be wondering how to get away with shooting him, not speculating about the bombshell he'd dropped earlier.

DHS agent Samuelson was Cael McCabe's father.

It was hard to wrap her mind around that. And even more difficult to keep questions from skirting the edges of her concentration, when she should be focused totally on de la Reyes.

But her mind kept creeping back like a thief in the night to worry at the pronouncement. Because there was a whole lot that Cael had left unsaid. Far more that Samuelson had neglected to mention than she'd originally believed.

Their relationship didn't explain—not by a long shot—the antipathy that apparently existed between the two men. Because if McCabe hated his father, it had been apparent at the meeting in Sanders's office that Samuelson harbored no tender feelings for Cael, either.

A knock sounded on the door then. De la Reyes looked up from his phone call as a guardsman poked his head inside, caught Ava's eye. She strode over to the half-opened door to watch as Vice President Quintero, his expression long-suffering, was frisked by two of the guardsmen. Satisfied, Ava nodded and the man was allowed to enter the room.

A moment later the president ended his phone call and got up to greet the man, before the two of them sat at the table in the far side of the room, conducting their business in undertones. Immediately her mind began to wander again.

She'd do well to stop contemplating the relationship and hatred between Samuelson and McCabe and start worrying about herself. About her son. Cael may have been exaggerating things to win her assistance, but she suspected there was a small kernel of truth in his professed concern for her. Namely that Samuelson would retaliate against her if she refused to help him. It wasn't difficult to believe that he'd learned of her father's identity.

There was a slight rise in voice level from the two men at the table, and Ava diverted her attention sharply, assessing the scene for possible risk. A moment later they were back to near whispers. Her instincts heightened, she pushed aside personal distractions to focus on the task at hand.

Although she wasn't yet sure how, she was going to make damn certain this whole thing didn't come back to touch Alex. Resolve steeled inside her. He'd sounded so shocked on the phone when she'd told him he had a grandfather. So angry when he'd accused her of lying. She'd refused to tell him her father's name yet. That couldn't be done over the phone. But when her son learned the truth it'd be from her. Not from Cael or Samuelson.

With dark humor, she considered that at least the earlier conversation with McCabe had forewarned her. She just needed to come up with a way to protect her son from a powerful government official and a dangerous ex-special ops soldier, in between the task of guarding the president of San Baltes with a shrinking security force.

Piece of cake.

"Miss Fuente has announced her plan to go out for an evening of nightclubbing." Cael's voice was carefully expressionless. "I've suggested to the president that it might be best that she not return, at least until we get a better handle on security here. He was initially reluctant, but eventually agreed."

The details of that particular conversation came as no surprise to Ava. She'd been within earshot of the heated exchange. Marissa had spent dinner arguing with de la Reyes about her "banishment."

"Our job," Cael stressed with noticeable inflection, "is to make sure the exit from the compound goes smoothly and that the guardsmen are aware the limo won't be allowed to reenter. We want to minimize our risks here." He looked at Sibbits. "You'll be on duty with Gonzalez so you won't be able to help us out with that. Benton will stay on shift with de la Reyes, but I'll update him on the plan." His gaze switched to Ava. "That leaves both of us to prepare the guardsmen on duty. You take the outer perimeter and I'll take the inner."

"So you want me to be sure the outside perimeter is clear before opening the gate for the limo. And ensure it doesn't get back inside until further notice." Cael's nod had satisfaction flickering. It wouldn't be a hardship to see the end of Fuente for a while. Ava wasn't sure how much longer she could take of the woman's baiting without decking her. "Any word from Reynolds?"

She could tell Cael's answer from his expression before his answer. "No." A muscle twitched in his jaw. "But there's nothing we can do about that until the rest of the team gets here."

She could read the concern behind the carefully dispassionate tone. Had the fleeting thought that it was only when his emotion was directed at her that she distrusted it.

"I had a conversation with Emmanuel Ortega earlier today," Cael informed him. "There are military teams covering every residence that Ramirez owns. They've turned some informants who are giving them valuable information about the man's operation. Once he has been neutralized the danger to de la Reyes will drastically decrease." He smiled humorlessly. "We just need to keep him alive in the meantime."

Ava wondered if she was the only one in the room unconvinced. If the government had known how to get to Ramirez, he'd have been arrested a long time ago, wouldn't he? Hopefully the informants could lead the way to the drug lord. At any rate, their job here hadn't gotten any easier.

Which made Fuente's upcoming departure the hands-down highlight of her day.

The woman was taking her sweet time. Ava consulted her watch. After nine thirty. She supposed the nightclub scene didn't get really started until much later. Hard to imagine someone wanting to spend a night in a bar full of drunks with an assault of earsplitting music, but she imagined Fuentes went more to be seen than anything else.

The limo had pulled up to the front entrance fifteen minutes ago. Ava had supervised the mandatory body search of the driver, which the man had endured good-naturedly. The vehicle had been cleared before being released to him. Protocol was being followed without a hitch so far. The driver had gone into the palace to retrieve Fuente's many bags, leaving the driver's and left passenger doors and trunk open. She'd lost count of the number of trips he'd made out to the waiting vehicle, taking great care to stow the bags in the trunk.

It occurred to her that someone had changed the tires on the car she'd shot out during its stay on the compound. She suspected that task had been left to the driver.

Ava spoke into her wrist transmitter. "Prepare for departure within fifteen."

"Inner perimeter, check." Cael's voice sounded on the radio. He must be in back of the palace, as he was out of sight.

"Outer perimeter, check." She recognized the voice of the guard at the gate she'd spoken to earlier.

She waited another few minutes, but neither the driver nor Fuente emerged. Rolling her eyes, she spoke into her wrist mike again. "Benton, are we prepared for departure?"

Her skin prickled in the ensuing silence. She heard Cael's voice next. "Benton, what's your—"

The rest of his words were lost as a mighty blast rocked the area, sending Ava sprawling.

Chapter 9

Disoriented, Ava rolled swiftly to her feet, her rifle in position. She half expected to see the palace engulfed in flames. Was momentarily confused to see it still standing, relatively unharmed.

In the next moment she saw the plumes of smoke rising in the distance from behind the palace and comprehension slammed into her.

Gonzalez's quarters had been triggered.

Fireballs hurtled like rockets skyward. She muttered an epithet and started running for the house. "Benton, what's your location?" she shouted into her mike.

"Maintain position." Cael's snapped order halted her progress. "I'm in a jeep right now heading toward the captain's quarters. Benton? Benton?"

After several moments, Cael spoke again. "Carter, check inside. See what the hell's going on."

But in the end she didn't follow that order. She didn't have to. Because the door to the front of the palace swung open. Dropping back, she took refuge in the meticulously landscaped bushes that surrounded the opulent structure.

The scene on the steps filled her veins with ice. Quietly, she spoke into her mike. "Limo driver is exiting side one, opening one. He's holding two weapons. One on de la Reyes. The other on Fuente."

"Do you have a shot?"

She sighted, felt a surge of frustration. "Not yet," she whispered back. "But I might get a clear head shot as they move past me toward the vehicle."

"If it's clear…take it."

A deadly calm settled over her. As silently as possible she inched farther back into the shrubs, sinking to a crouch. All she had to do was wait. Ignore the pound and spike of adrenaline and calm her speeding pulse. Give the man time to head to the limo. Once there he was faced with placing two captives in the car. The diversion might provide the clearest target.

A head shot was her only option. Breathing deeply, Ava kept her mind clear of everything but the task before her. With his weapons trained on the two captives, her only chance of avoiding a reflex shot from the driver would be to sever his brain stem. She didn't doubt her ability if the opportunity arose. She'd had plenty of practice. But first she needed the driver to walk down those stairs. Take several steps toward the vehicle.

He spoke loudly in Spanish. "Weapons down. Pile them at the base of the porch. Or your president is dead."

With a sinking heart, Ava watched as one by one the guardsmen in the vicinity lowered their weapons. Moved slowly to add their rifles and handguns to the growing pile.

"You two." He singled out a couple of guardsmen. "Take all of them and throw them in the fountain. Your obedience is all that is keeping de la Reyes alive."

Move. Just down the steps, you bastard, Ava urged silently.

Let's see what you're made of when you're not the only one armed.

"Where is Carter? I want her out here now! Throw your weapons down and hands in the air." Translating effortlessly, Ava remained hidden, her mind wheeling with alternatives. The driver had seen her earlier. He knew she'd been out here the entire time he'd waited. But he couldn't be sure she remained here after the explosion, could he?

She sighted again, silently cursing the way he held both hostages close to him, with the muzzles of his weapons pressed against their temples.

"I'll shoot Fuente first," the man promised in his native tongue. As if on cue, the woman stopped sobbing and began to scream. "Throw down your weapons, Carter. I will give you three seconds before I shoot her. One."

Coolly, she weighed her options. De la Reyes seemed frozen, but she couldn't see his expression. If the driver pulled the trigger, the crumpling of Fuente's body would provide the clear shot she needed.

"Two."

But the man hadn't progressed any farther down the steps. Which meant her only shot was above the ear, taking the chance the bullet could pass through his skull and into de la Reyes's.

"Three…"

"I'm here," she shouted. Lowering her rifle, she rose, feeling supremely vulnerable. Her handgun was holstered across her chest, easily visible. She was otherwise unarmed.

"Step out where I can see you. Keep your hands up!"

She obeyed, circling the porch as she emerged, waiting for an opportunity to dive for cover and take a shot if it should present itself.

"Disarm her," he instructed the guardsmen nearby.

None of them moved.

"Disarm her, or one of them dies now."

Slowly, reluctantly, a guard moved toward her. His face was grim as he took her rifle. Unholstered her Luger.

"They go in the fountain, too." After the order, the driver looked at her, his expression cocky. "We do not want to chance having Carter shoot our tires out again, do we? Where is McCabe?"

Ava was wondering the same thing. Her wrist transmitter was on. If he was listening, he should hear enough of the scene to have him heading back.

The question was whether he'd back in time to make a difference.

"He went to check out the explosion site. That's what you intended, wasn't it? To divide us?"

"Get up here," the man instructed in Spanish.

Warily, Ava remained where she was. "Why?"

"Now!"

It's what she didn't see in his expression that had her moving forward. There was no fear. No reservation. This man would kill without hesitation.

Once she was on the porch, he ordered her to take up position several feet behind him. With a sinking feeling in her stomach, she did so. "Stay back that far, but follow us to the limo."

Fuente had subsided to wild keening noises as she stumbled alongside the driver. Ava did as ordered, following them from a short distance, scanning the tableau around her.

The guardsmen seemed frozen. A few of them looked at her, as if for guidance. She gave a short shake of her head. There was nothing any of them could do that wouldn't put the president at risk.

McCabe, however…if he'd returned from the captain's quarters… if he were in the vicinity…he might try for a shot.

How good a marksman was he? Ava wasn't sure. It took well over average skill to make a head shot. It took outstanding skill and luck to make it without killing a hostage as close as de la Reyes and Fuente were to the gunman.

Her stomach plummeting, she recognized they were short on both.

The gunman shoved Fuente toward the open passenger door. *"Entrar."* She scrambled in, for once lacking the grace and dignity she usually displayed. The driver nudged de la Reyes toward the driver's seat and Ava silently cursed. A driver presented a constant target. But the gunman would be hiding low in the seat. Still a danger to the hostages he'd taken.

But providing no shot.

The gunman ordered de la Reyes to close his door, and the president obeyed. Then he turned to Ava and shouted in Spanish, "If a car follows, they die. If I hear a helicopter overhead, they die." With one gun still trained on the president, he slammed the door. A moment later the limo began to move.

Ava got one last look of de la Reyes as he slowly drove by.

He looked like a man going to his death.

"He says Benton must go to the hospital."

"Bullshit," the operative said weakly from the couch he was lying on in the president's private quarters. "Tell the quack to patch me up and I'll be good to go."

The presidential physician looked at Ava expectantly. But it was Cael she was watching.

"Ask him what a hospital can do that he can't do right here."

Without relaying his question she responded, "He should go." Ignoring the weak protest her words brought from Benton, she continued. "This isn't a war zone where you slap on a field dressing and call it good. He could have internal damage. And there's nothing he can do here."

"The hell there isn't!"

This time it was Cael ignoring the man. "Okay."

"McCabe, come on. This isn't necessary." The doctor waved two white-clothed medics to lift Benton's makeshift gurney and carry him toward the door. "McCabe!"

Ava gestured to the man at her side, speaking rapidly to

the doctor. *"Y ahora usted necesita mirarlo. Vea como es serio sus quemaduras son y los tratan."*

As the man came toward him, Cael looked at her warily. "What'd you tell him?"

"That your burns need to be treated."

"I'm fine."

"Yeah." She didn't bother hiding her skepticism. "You look fine." He looked, in fact, like he'd emerged from the depths of hell. His hair was singed, and so was one eyebrow. Black soot covered every bare inch of skin, except the patches on his arms and one palm that were pink and oozing.

The doctor told her in Spanish, "He must wash. Dirt is the worst thing for a burn. Then I can treat him."

"You need to shower." Queasiness filled her just thinking of the pain he must be in. "Then he can put ointment on the burns."

The expression on his face was fierce. "We've got a helluva bonfire south of the palace and the president has been kidnapped from under our noses. The vice president will be here at any minute. I've got a little more to deal with than a few scrapes."

"Not being treated isn't going to put the fire out or get de la Reyes and Fuente back. And the vice president isn't here yet," she replied calmly. "Standing around acting macho is stupid and accomplishes nothing. Risking infection is even dumber. So give me your room key. I'll go fetch some clothes for you while you shower and let the doctor treat you." There was a gleam in his pale green gaze that spelled danger. Ignoring it, she cocked a brow. "I'll let you take it from there."

He was silent a moment, his eyes searching. Then he gave a short nod. "I've got a plan."

Adrenaline, recently tamped, flickered to life again. "You always do."

An hour later Ava was seated at a table next to Cael, who was dressed in a fresh T-shirt and fatigues. Vice President

Quintero sat opposite them, his expression grim as he listened to their terse recital of the events of the evening.

"I alerted Ortega at Justice to track down the identity and affiliations of the limo driver," he said in English after they'd finished. "But I don't understand where he got the weapons. It was your job to protect Antonio. The man should have been searched. He should have been—"

"He was," Ava said flatly. "I oversaw it myself. He had no weapons on him when he drove the car up to the front of the palace. The vehicle was clean, too."

"Then I do not understand—"

"He may have stolen them from the barracks and secreted them inside the palace. Hell, he may have bribed one of the guardsmen to do it for him. It would be easy enough then to retrieve them when he was carrying out the luggage."

Ava had her own suspicion on the matter, but decided to remain quiet for now. It was all supposition at this point, anyway. "At any rate, he had the weapons the third trip he made up for the luggage, because that's when he shot Benton and marched de la Reyes and Fuente down the stairs and out the door."

"And no one could stop him." It was clear Quintero wanted to blame someone for the president's disappearance. "All the armed security, and your team, Mr. McCabe...and no one could shoot this bastard when he was standing right in front of you!"

"Have you ever tried to sever a man's brain stem when he's holding two hostages on either side of him?" Ava asked evenly. "It's a tricky shot. I've accomplished it a few times, but I have to have a position behind the gunman. The target didn't expose himself. I assumed you'd prefer I didn't risk blowing away the top of the president's skull in the process. Maybe I was wrong about that."

The vice president opened his mouth. Shut it again.

Cael put in, "I called you immediately as things were going down. Did you contact the military?"

Quintero nodded. "The espionage plane was dispatched as

you requested. As you suspected, the limo was abandoned a few miles away and the president and Miss Fuente then were transported by a Land Rover. The vehicle entered the jungle southeast of here."

Ava's gaze jerked to Cael's. He looked unsurprised. "I'm confident they'll keep de la Reyes alive, at least for now. But your government should expect a communication from the rebels."

"You are more confident that I am myself." The man's tone was heated. "Ramirez has tried assassination before. What makes you think Antonio isn't already dead?"

"If Ramirez wanted him dead, he'd have been shot here," Cael said simply. "The fact that they bothered to take him means they need him alive, at least for a while."

The vice president frowned. "But why? What has changed that he…" Comprehension dawned on his face. "The frozen assets."

"Exactly." Cael nodded. "Only the president can order Ramirez's assets to be unfrozen, so it follows that he'll be allowed to live until he does so. However, once Ramirez can drain his accounts, de la Reyes is dead. So we don't have much time."

Stiffly, Quintero said, "There is no we, Mr. McCabe. I will take over from here. Already I have the military preparing rescue teams to go into the jungle."

"That would be a mistake."

The man's earlier politeness, Ava noted, had disappeared in the face of Cael's bluntness. "Many mistakes have been made here today, but none of them were mine." Cael reached for a rolled-up bunch of maps he'd been perusing before Quintero had arrived. Choosing one, he laid it out, tracing an area on it with his finger. "You have approximately ten thousand square miles of jungle in San Baltes. It would take hundreds of men weeks to cover all of it. You have a matter of days, not weeks, to get your president out safely."

"And what would you have us do in that time? Nothing at all?"

"You might talk to your minister of finance about ways to bog down the unfreezing of assets," Ava suggested. From Cael's look of approval she knew they were on the same track. "You also may pretend that there's a breakdown of communication within the government in the president's absence. Inter-cabinet bickering. Anything that will buy the president some time." Because one thing was clear. The moment Ramirez got his hands on his money, de la Reyes would be dead.

Folding his arms over his chest, Quintero said tersely, "This is all well and good. But how will the president be rescued if you say the military should not go looking for him?"

"That's easy enough," Cael said evenly. "I'm going in myself."

"You can't seriously be considering going in alone." Ava matched Cael stride for stride down the hallway to his room.

"Actually I'm through considering."

She eyed the patches on his arms covering the burns he'd sustained earlier that day. Delirium from pain might be responsible for such a risky illogical move, but he looked far from delirious. Determined. Lethal. But no less dangerous for his injuries.

"You can't even be sure where he's being held."

"The fact that he was taken into the jungle is a pretty big clue," he said dryly. They were at his door now. He unlocked it and pushed it open.

She followed him inside, an argument still on her lips. "You're thinking he's been taken to the rebel camp Reynolds located."

"Seems logical." He went to the closet in the room and pulled out a duffel bag, from which he extracted a backpack. Unrolling it, he tossed it on the bed. Then he went to the dresser and started pulling drawers open.

"You said yourself they change camp locations frequently."

Swiftly he crossed back to the bed with some clothes. Another pair of black fatigues. An extra tank undershirt. Several pairs of socks. A couple of changes of underwear. Ava averted her eyes. She definitely didn't need a mental picture of McCabe wearing only those dark briefs emblazoned on her mind.

But it was already too late. The image wouldn't be easily extricated.

"You could give the map Reynolds gave you to the military. What do you think you can accomplish that they can't?"

"I can not screw it up. I can't be sure they won't."

It was annoying to have to talk to his back. Now he was on the way to the adjoining bathroom, gathering up a toothbrush and paste.

"I'm sure they have trained professionals for just this sort of—"

"Are you?" His interruption cut her short. He paced back into the room and dropped the objects into the bag. "Because I'm not. I have no idea what this country's military capabilities are. How could I? I don't know if they have active recon and special ops teams or how well they're trained. I also don't know if Ramirez has someone embedded in the military reporting to him. What I am certain of is that it isn't worth taking the chance. I'm going in alone. Once I've located the camp and come up with a plan for getting our people out, I'll radio the military for backup, just like I told Quintero."

Ava felt a compelling desire to bounce something off his thick head. He wasn't being reasonable, and every protest seemed to slide off him. "At least take Sibbits. You trust him, right? Between the two of you…" Cael had gone still and an awful feeling of certainty came over her. Followed with a flood of sorrow. "Oh God."

Because of course the man had been on guard at Gonzalez's quarters. And no one standing that close to the house when it went off would have survived it.

Without conscious thought she closed the distance between them, laid her hand gently on his arm between the gauze bandages. "I'm so sorry, Cael."

She saw his throat working. The muscles in his jaw were clenched tight. But she wasn't prepared for the arm that snaked around her waist. Pulling her tightly against him.

He held her there, his face pressed against her hair, and she could feel his heart thudding against hers. Imagined she could feel the heaviness in it. "Ah…shit," he muttered. His arms held her so tightly she could scarcely breathe. And it seemed completely natural to slide her own around his waist and hug him, as if from the pressure she could release some of the pent-up emotion he was holding in.

It seemed like a long time before he spoke again. "It was like something out of hell. I knew it was him when I started to the quarters. Like a human torch, rolling around to put out the flames. I couldn't help him. When I finally got the flames out, he was…"

"I know." It was easy enough now to guess how he'd gotten those burns on his arms. She could imagine the scene vividly. And her heart ached. Both for the fallen operative and for the man who couldn't save him. And the grief he bore because of it. The muscles in his shoulders were trembling under the weight of sorrow. And she wanted, quite simply, to wipe it away. To relieve him of the burden of remorse that she knew he'd carry to the end of his days.

She understood what it was to fail. To watch in horror and misery as an assignment spun horribly out of control. She'd seen hostage takers do their worst before she could get a clear shot. Seen strung-out estranged husbands do unspeakable things to the women they claimed to love while children stood in petrified terror as the scene unfolded before them.

Ava had been part of far more successful missions than not, but it was the ones that went wrong that haunted her. So she knew what Cael was going through. And realized there was nothing to say that would ease his pain.

They stood like that for several minutes, fused together in a way that had nothing to do with passion and everything to do with the very human need for comfort. She didn't wonder—not then—what it was about the man that stripped her defenses so easily. Touched her emotions so deftly.

When he spoke his face was still resting lightly on her hair. His voice was muffled. "I won't lose another one." He took a breath and released her. "I figure there's a chance Perez and Reynolds will be there, too. They've been the most exposed of any of us. They were on the ground before we arrived and they've spent the most time outside the palace compound. Ramirez may have learned their identities. It's still fairly common down here for foreign contractors or their family members to be kidnapped and held for ransom. They might be in the same place the rebels are keeping de la Reyes and Fuente."

Because it seemed cruel, she didn't point out the obvious. That they could just as easily be killed as spies if captured. That they might already be dead.

"What good will you be doing anyone if you get caught yourself?" she asked in a shaky voice.

"I won't."

"You can't know that!" Ava stopped, unsure where the fervor in her voice had stemmed from. When she was sure she'd calmed it, she tried again. "At least take a couple of the soldiers. You have a better chance if you're not in there alone."

"I never go into battle with someone I can't trust. Better to go alone than to have to watch my back the entire time."

Her breath seemed strangled in her lungs. She stared at him with futile frustration. He acted as though he were inde-structible, but just the opposite was true. He had the bandages on his arms to prove it.

"I have to go." He checked his watch. "If Ramirez is expecting someone to come after them, they'll be easier to evade while it's still dark."

"All right." A numbed sort of acceptance had come over her. "Give me ten minutes to pack. I'm coming with you."

Chapter 10

"You can let me out here," Cael told Vasquez tersely.

"You can let both of us out here."

The look Cael threw Ava was blistering. She pretended not to notice. Opening the door of the jeep, she got out and reached in for her pack, shrugging into it. Then she slipped the rifle strap over her head and straightened.

It had taken longer than the ten minutes she'd promised before she'd been ready to leave the palace. But that was only because Cael had spent half an hour alternating between arguing and pleading with her to see reason. His anger now was just as ineffectual. She wasn't letting him go into this kind of danger alone. He needed someone at his back, even if that someone was suppressing an increasingly strong urge to brain him with one of her boots.

The night was lit by a slice of whitewashed moon pinned low in the sky. The hem of the jungle loomed across the road at the foothills of the mountains, its depths dark and unwelcoming. Its canopy would shut out any illumination from above.

A chill skittered over her skin. Cael had no idea just how little she wanted to enter it with him. Or how determined she was to do just that.

It wouldn't do to examine her reasons too closely. Given his plans for her future once back in the States, she certainly didn't owe him any favors. And if it occurred to her that her problems would be over if he didn't return from the jungle, the thought brought panic, not relief.

So she was going in. She'd deal with the future later.

He was glaring at her now, temper radiating off him in waves.

"I only go on missions with people I trust. You certainly don't qualify."

"Given your attitude, you *shouldn't* trust me. I'm ready to punch you already."

"You can still go back with Vasquez. Supervise the handling of Ramirez's demands."

"You're wasting time." She walked by him, across the lonely strip of deserted gravel road. Ava was fairly certain she could hear him grinding his teeth behind her.

A quick muttered conversation sounded behind her. Then a few moments later he caught up with her. Passed her.

"Stay behind me," he snapped, fixing the goggles over his eyes. "And for chrissakes try to move quietly."

The sound of the jeep driving away gave her a momentary flicker of panic. But in the next minute she squared her shoulders and plunged into the jungle behind him, adjusting her own night-vision goggles.

It was slow going at first. Cael hacked and sawed at strangler vines to clear a path for them. He'd clear a foot and then stop and begin sawing again. She wondered silently how they would ever make time if they had to do this the whole way. But after several yards the ground cleared even as the trees crowded in, effectively closing around them.

The goggles lit the blackness to an eerie green. She concentrated on keeping her footsteps silent and remained as close to Cael as she dared. The sudden screech that sounded above her nearly had her jumping on his back.

"Shit!" She remembered, barely, to whisper.

"Howler monkey." His voice sounded laconically ahead of her. "They can raise a heckuva racket."

For the first time she became aware of the night sounds playing all around them. She could hear the deep croak of frogs, and in the distance a coughing sound she thought would belong to some sort of big cat. A jaguar? Every once in a while there'd come a faint animal scream, as predator vanquished prey.

She hoped they'd escape the same fate.

After they'd been on the move about a half hour Cael abruptly stopped. He slipped off the bag he wore on his back easily, although she guessed it weighed a good forty pounds. Going down on one knee, he opened it and withdrew something, which he handed to her. "I'm going to let you hang on to this. Turn it on, but keep the light pointed downward."

Ava snapped on the heavy mag light and saw him take something from his pocket, smooth it out on the ground before them. She recognized the map Reynolds had brought back of the rebel camp. He spent several minutes studying the coordinates and comparing them with the wrist GPS he wore. Finally he rose, folding the map back up and tucking it away. "We need to start adjusting our path a bit to the west, but we should reach the camp within a few hours."

Without waiting for his directive, she switched off the light and fell in behind him as he started to move again. "It'll be full light by then."

"We'll get as close as we can and remain hidden. Wait for night for a full recon. See what we're dealing with."

Ava waved away a mosquito roughly the size of a Volkswagen. "I can already answer that. Based on Reynolds's estimate, we're going to be dealing with at least a hundred-to-one odds."

"Not necessarily." It seemed curiously intimate to be alone

together in the darkness, conducting a conversation in near whispers. "If Reynolds and Perez are there with de la Reyes and Fuente, it'd be closer to thirty-five to one."

The mention of the woman's name reminded her of something. "About Fuente…I don't think the limo driver was acting alone."

He stopped so suddenly she ran into the back of him. "Will you stop doing that?"

"You have reason to suspect her?"

"I never saw the driver near the house, did you? When would he have had the opportunity to hide weapons in there?"

"Where would she have gotten her hands on weapons?" She barely could make out his head shake as he began moving again. "She's hardly the type."

Ava rolled her eyes. Men could be unbelievably obtuse about women sometimes. "She got her hands on a remote, didn't she? Think about it. If the driver is working for Ramirez, what reason would he have for killing Gonzalez?"

"Maybe Gonzalez failed in whatever Ramirez hired him for. Or maybe he just doesn't like loose ends. He might have believed the man was going to talk since we had him dead to rights on the deposits. And you have to admit." His voice turned bleak. "Triggering his quarters was a hell of a distraction."

"Something about Fuente's reaction didn't ring true," she insisted stubbornly. Aside from her dislike for the woman, there was something there she hadn't trusted from the first. "When the driver had her and the president on the porch she was crying and carrying on. But remember how she acted that first night when the limo was surrounded by armed guards and I had a gun on her? She wasn't scared, she was furious and disdainful. Where was the fury this evening?"

A woman like Marissa Fuente had an air of entitlement that would make it difficult to believe anything bad could befall her or those she cared about. If Ava had to guess which was the woman's real persona, she'd pick the haughty one, not the

sobbing, trembling woman who had crawled into the back of
the limo seat. "There was no reason to take Fuente along. He
had the president. Two hostages are harder to control than one.
I think she's in on it."

"And I think you're letting those scratches she left you with
color your perception." Ironically, there was a note of humor
in his voice. "I don't think she'd have any part of endanger-
ing de la Reyes. She seems to be in love with him."

The words were jarring, coming from him. "I never would
have pegged you for a romantic."

"Hardly. Any illusions I had about most people's intentions
became pretty jaded at an early age."

Her mind returned to the bombshell he'd dropped—was it
only yesterday? "By your father?"

Cael's stride seemed to grow longer. His voice more terse.
"He's not my father in any way but biological. He wasn't in
my life until I was fourteen."

There was that familiar bitterness tingeing his tone. And
for once, Ava was determined she'd hear the origin of the antipathy between the two men. "You resented him for not being
around when you were growing up?"

He was silent so long she didn't think he'd answer. When
he did, his voice was flat. "I resented him for coming back. But
not right away. At first I watched how happy my mother was.
She'd never married. Had always refused to name my father,
too. I have her name. But I knew when I saw them together
that she'd never stopped loving him. I worshiped my mother.
But she was blind when it comes to Dennis Samuelson."

"How long did he stay this time?"

"Long enough to convince her to take me to the hospital
for a tissue match. Seems he had another son. Two years
older than me, with the wife he must have been married to
even when I was conceived. A real prince, that guy is. John,
his son, had liver cancer. His parents weren't matches. He had
no other siblings."

But he'd had a half brother. The sick realization filled her. She could already imagine what had brought Samuelson back to the woman and child he'd abandoned. And it hadn't been some long-awaited familial devotion. "He convinced your mother to have you tested."

"He didn't have to. By the time he was done with the whole sad story—a story that glossed right over the details of the wife he'd lied to her about—my mother offered. I didn't really know what to expect but I went along with it. And I was a match."

Something swooped low, almost touching her shoulder, and Ava ducked defensively. Although there were few things she hated as much as bats, her mind was elsewhere. "So he should be grateful to you. The surgery was successful?"

"At first. And I can see now, looking back, that Samuelson was already edging his way out of our lives as John looked like he was recovering. But months later his body rejected the transplant. He died a year after the operation."

"He was in and out of our lives after that. My mother grew increasingly distraught when she wouldn't hear from him for months at a time." His voice was heavy with irony. "Of course he never left contact information. Watch out here."

She nearly missed the shift in conversation. It was at the last second that she ducked beneath the heavy vine he was holding out of the way for her. "What brought him back after that? I mean…"

"After he'd abandoned us once?" Cael was quiet for a moment, wondering why he was bothering to tell her all this. It was ancient history. Belaboring it had never solved anything. "I suppose for a short time he entertained notions of molding his remaining son into a copy of himself. That didn't happen." He'd been a smart-ass kid with a mile wide chip on his shoulder toward the man who consistently wreaked havoc in their lives. The more Samuelson pushed, the more Cael had resisted. And it wasn't long before they discovered that they hated each other's guts.

"He left for good the summer I graduated. I was determined to join the navy. He was just as determined to pull strings and get me into West Point. My mother sided with him. But I was eighteen and didn't need parental permission. I left anyway. He never went back to my mother after that." And Cael would always blame the man for his mother's eventual suicide. The familiar bitterness lodged in his throat, threatening to choke him.

He cleared his throat. "He resurfaced several times over the years, mostly to throw a wrench into whatever plans I had going on." He'd damn near kept Cael out of the SEALs. Would have, if his commanding officer hadn't shared Cael's disdain for bureaucratic bullshit. "He was actually pretty high in military intelligence at the time. When he decided to tamper, he could usually get results."

The man had managed, over the years, to get Cael assigned to more than his share of high-risk missions. He wasn't sure what he'd been hoping for, that he'd screw up or get himself killed. But he'd never minded in one sense. That was why he'd become a SEAL. And he'd gotten experience fast, built a reputation for being a solid soldier more swiftly than most. Cael figured his survival was the best way to get back at the old man.

"He contacted me once more, after I didn't reenlist last time. Tried to get me to dish dirt on the military commanders I'd had. Missions I'd been involved in that hadn't gone according to plan. I told him to go…" He amended the sentence in the last possible moment. "To forget it. He offered to get me a job working military intelligence reporting to him. I turned him down flat. Told him I was going to start my own company."

"When did he join DHS?"

"Almost at its inception. And believe me, his position gives him plenty of opportunity to make trouble. We've seen his hand in more than a couple of deadly turns an assignment has taken. He wouldn't mind seeing me dead. But barring that, he wants to see me ruined or in prison. The way he sees it, the wrong son died. He won't be happy until he's erased a part of his past that he doesn't care to remember." Their voices were low and wouldn't travel far. But he never stopped assessing the jungle around them.

Their surroundings offered ample hiding places, but he didn't expect to see rebel guards posted this far out. Not until they got closer to the camp would there be a need for an outer perimeter.

They walked for a couple more hours, mostly in silence, stopping only to check the map and coordinates. He hadn't meant to tell her the whole pathetic story of how Samuelson had screwed over his family. But maybe now she'd recognize the man for what he was. Realize that returning to the States carried its own kind of danger. One he still hadn't figured a way for her to avoid if she continued to refuse the one plan he did have.

And there was no use asking if she'd changed her mind about that. If there was one thing he'd learned about the woman, it was that she was immovable once she'd made a decision.

"Let's take a water break." He drank from his water bottle and figured she was digging in her pack for hers. But instead she pulled out a small bottle and started spraying the contents on her hands. Rubbing them on her face and neck.

"What are you doing?"

"Reapplying bug repellent."

He nodded. His own hadn't provided as much protection as he'd hoped against the mosquitoes and flies they'd encountered. "Mud's probably the best protection. We can scoop up handfuls of it and rub it on any exposed area. Not too appealing, but it works."

"I prefer my repellent. I haven't been bitten yet."

That stopped him in midswallow. "You haven't been bitten?"

"Nope."

"Gimme that."

She handed over the bottle and he brought it to his nose, sniffed suspiciously. "What is this? It smells all girly."

"It may have escaped your attention," she drawled, "but I am female."

"Believe me, that has never escaped my attention." There were many times over the last several days when he would have given anything to forget it. He sniffed again, wrestled briefly between the two choices, shrugged. What the hell? It would wear off. He spread a liberal amount on himself before handing it back to her. "Give me the flashlight, would you?"

When she did so, he switched it on aiming the beam at the map he'd spread out on the jungle floor. "It's nearly dawn."

"What?"

He heard the surprise in Ava's voice. The secondary canopy of the trees would block out any light that managed to filter through, at least until full day. "It's four-thirty. And by my estimates we're only an hour away from the camp. We'll need to be more careful from here on in. No talking. I'm guessing they'll have guards posted on the outer perimeter maybe as far as an hour from the camp." If the president was being held there, more precautions would be taken than normal. "We need to do a recon before we go any further."

"And exactly what does that entail?"

He grinned at the suspicion in her tone. "How are you at climbing trees?"

She was silent behind him for a moment. Then, "As long as it's free of howler monkeys, I can manage."

He didn't tell her the monkeys were the least of her worries. It was the snakes and slug rats she'd need to watch out for.

"You'll get a visual from above. Once we're in sight of the camp I'll get closer on the ground. We'll use the whisper mics to communicate. We need to get a visual of the layout and more importantly, location of all posted guards and their scheduled rotation. Get a count of the hostages and the soldiers."

A thought then had him cursing. "I only brought one pair of field glasses."

"I packed a pair."

A measure of respect tangled with pride filtered through. Of course. She'd probably packed as carefully as he had.

He checked the trees carefully, continuing on until he found one that would work. It had to be large enough that it towered above the secondary canopy, or she wouldn't be able to see anything anyway. One with stout vines would be best, so she could walk her way up the side of the trunk to the limbs.

"I'll hold your rifle."

She slipped the strap off her neck and handed it to him while donning the binoculars she'd taken out of the pack she left at the bottom of the tree.

Cael laid the rifle against a nearby tree and grabbed a vine, yanked on it testingly. "It should hold your weight. But take this with you." He handed her the sheath containing the large bladed knife he'd been using to clear their path when they'd started that night.

Ava looked at him and then at him. Her eyes narrowed suspiciously. "What do I need that for?"

"It's just a precaution in case you disturb someone's home."

"Why do I have a feeling there's something you're not telling me?" she muttered. But she buckled the knife belt around her waist.

"You might see a toucan. Or a macaw."

"Uh-huh. What else lives in these trees? No, don't tell me." She took the vine from him and placed both booted feet against the huge trunk, leaning her weight back to keep the vine taut. Then, with an athletic grace that had him blinking in astonishment, she scrambled up the side and disappeared into the low-hanging branches.

He waited for what seemed an interminable amount of time, but was probably no more than ten minutes. While he waited, he consulted the map again. Then her voice sounded in his mic. "I've got a good view but I don't see the camp. I'm coming down." A few moments later he heard a rustling sound and something came whizzing down at him, in two pieces.

Cael ducked out of the way and the things thudded to the ground. Bending closer to check it out, he grimaced distastefully and moved away. At least the woman knew what to do when she encountered a slug rat.

A couple of minutes later he could see her making her way carefully down the tree again. Her long, slender legs encased in the dark fatigues were scrabbling for purchase as she slowly lowered herself to a branch that would support her weight.

Cael found a stout vine and walked it around the trunk until it was within arm's reach of her. Then Ava grasped it and descended the trunk, as easily as she'd walked up it.

The look in her eye when she stalked toward him was lethal. "I have a little bone to pick with you, McCabe."

"Ah…" If he smiled he'd be as dead as the slug rat. "I guess you didn't see a toucan."

She gave him a shove. "Next time you do the visual from the air and I'll take my chances with the guards."

He did grin then, earning himself another push. "You're lighter. Better chance of the branches holding your weight. And I'll admit it, I'm more practiced on the ground."

He handed her weapon back to her, noted that she didn't offer to return the knife.

"Just remember, I owe you one."

Cael continued onward. He was certain that before this mission was over, she'd find a way to repay him. In spades.

Fifteen minutes later they repeated the process, minus the dead slug rat. And fifteen minutes after that, Ava shimmied up another tree, with a noticeable lack of enthusiasm, while Cael worried beneath it. They had to be getting close. If she wasn't getting a view, maybe he should…

"I can see it from here."

His attention jerked to the sound of her voice in his mic. "How far?"

"Couple miles. They just cut down newer vegetation to make a good-sized clearing. Blends right in."

It took effort to keep his voice even as he asked, "Do you see the hostages?"

There was silence for a minute. Two. Then Ava's voice sounded again. "I don't see live hostages. Cael, I don't see anyone. I think the camp has been abandoned."

Chapter 11

Ava remained silent as they walked through the makeshift camp. Cael's expression was grim. The rebels hadn't moved hastily. There was nothing left behind but trash. No food supplies. No weapons.

Just flies buzzing over four bodies.

She'd held her breath while he turned each of them over. Felt vaguely guilty at the relief she felt each time she didn't recognize a victim. They'd been hostages at one time, that was clear. Each was still bound. And riddled with bullet holes.

Sickened, she turned away. She couldn't allow herself to wonder if the same fate awaited the newest hostages.

The makeshift buildings were constructed of the saplings and trees they'd cut down. But there were other structures consisting of similar young trees sharpened into points and pounded into the ground. She knew without asking that the structures had served as cells.

"They've been gone a couple days, I'd guess."

She looked at Cael askance. "How can you possibly know when they left?"

"Without getting too graphic, I checked the decomposition on the bodies." He shrugged, his gaze sweeping the area. "Good news is if they are holding the hostages, they probably aren't located that far away. No more than a few hours, anyway. Probably sent a team ahead to prepare a new camp and moved out when it was ready."

"And we're going to follow them." He didn't have to say the words. Ava was beginning to know the man very well indeed.

"Shouldn't be too hard. A hundred or more people moving through a jungle are going to leave a trail. And they moved out recently enough that the vegetation won't have hidden the path they took yet."

Ava was amazed, however, at just how faint the trail appeared in spots. It had been easy enough to see which direction the camp occupants had followed. But there were places where they had to stop so Cael could search for traces of the faint trail. She imagined the shadowy confines of the jungle would swallow up their own path in mere days. The lush vegetation sprawled everywhere. It was humans who were the trespassers here.

The sun slanted in wherever it could pierce the double canopy above them. But that didn't affect the humidity. By midmorning Ava had sweat through her clothes and had a constant stream of perspiration running down her neck. The backpack seemed to grow heavier with each step she took.

She was in good shape. The department's annual fitness test was never a problem. But hiking through a jungle in a tropical climate tested her in ways the department obstacle course didn't begin to. The heat turned the jungle into a steamy sauna, and it was sapping more energy by the second.

They stopped every half hour to find a tree and see if she could get a visual of the new camp. Each time she scrambled down to report in the negative. To her relief, she didn't encounter another of the disgusting creatures she'd killed this morning, but did disturb a gibbon once, which gave an ear-splitting screech before it swung to a nearby tree and continued its tirade from there.

She also learned more than she'd ever wanted about the slime mold that grew up some tree trunks. Distaste filled her at the memory of her earlier encounter with it.

Wiping her dripping forehead on the long sleeve of the shirt she wore, she slanted a look at Cael. He seemed tireless. His unshaven jaw was bristled with whiskers a couple of shades darker than the hair on his head. He had a black bandana wrapped around his forehead keeping his hair out of his eyes. And his clothes were as soaked as hers were.

Mutinously, she stopped, glaring at his back. "You might be powered by Everready batteries, but some of us need an occasional break, Attila."

He looked back over his shoulder, his expression impatient. A moment later there was a visible thawing in it and he turned to head swiftly back to her. "You're right. We need fuel and we have to stay hydrated." Rejoining her, he slipped out of his pack and set it down. She did the same, restraining a moan of relief when she got rid of its weight.

She cut a couple of ferns and laid them down on the ground before collapsing on them with little grace. "Last time I got a visual I could hear water nearby." Just the sound had uncorked a yearning to find it and submerge herself in it. Her last shower was a distant memory. It helped to imagine that any body of water would be as suspect as some of the other things she'd encountered in the jungle.

"Must be a creek or small falls nearby." He was checking the coordinates again, his head down. "Might be a good place to hide out later, if the camp isn't too much further."

She swallowed. Once they found the camp, they'd need to do surveillance before retiring to make a rescue plan.

Ava didn't even want to think of what the odds were of them

succeeding. Instead she pulled her pack toward her, unzipped it and started rummaging around in it. "Want a sandwich?"

"When did you have time to make those?" He took the food readily enough, though, unwrapping it to bite into the thick ham between toasted buns.

"I didn't. I called down to the kitchen while I was packing and had them prepare some and send them up." She took a bite of her own sandwich and washed it down with a large gulp of water. The heat sapped the liquid from her body almost as soon as she drank each time. But at least that meant she didn't have to stop and pee very frequently, for which she was decidedly grateful.

"Beats the field rations I brought," he agreed, devouring the sandwich in a few bites.

"Why would you bring…" She stopped midsentence, and watched a brilliant blue butterfly the size of her fist flutter in back of his shoulder into the thick vegetation. It was like being in a different world, she reflected. And certainly it was as far removed from her experience as it was possible to be.

"Habit. Never occurred to me to raid the kitchen." He took a long pull from his water bottle. "But they don't take up much space, and after your food is gone you'll be happy enough to have them."

She'd brought a dozen sandwiches. Ava was sincerely hoping they'd be safely back at the palace before their provisions gave out. But since their safe return seemed rather dicey at the moment, she said nothing.

Their long dark clothing made it seem hotter than it was. But, as Cael had explained hours ago, it was a mistake to bare any more skin than necessary in the jungle. And so far Ava was inclined to agree. She'd reapplied repellent several more times, but mosquitoes and other stinging insects still swarmed and lighted, even if she had managed to avoid being devoured so far.

"As long as we're stopped we may as well change your bandages."

He shook his head. "They're fine."

"They need to be changed daily and be kept dry. Given the state of our clothing, they're probably soaked." From her pack she took out a plastic bag filled with the medical supplies the doctor had left behind for him.

He stared at her, arrested. "What all do you have in that pack?"

"I'm sure the contents are much more innocent than what you're carrying," she said dryly. She looked up from her preparations quizzically. "You'll need to lose the shirt."

His eyes remained fixed on hers, heated. Silently he started working buttons through buttonholes. An answering warmth suffused her, one that owed nothing to the humidity.

There was nothing remotely sexy about their situation. Or her request. But that didn't stop her pulse from churning to a faster pace with every button he released. It didn't stop her throat from drying, despite the drink she'd just taken. And it didn't prevent her imagination from painting this as a strip-tease, rather than just as a matter of first aid.

The shirt was completely undone now and he was working on the cuffs. Because it seemed safer, Ava busied herself tearing open the packages of gauze pads, being careful not to expose any portion of them to possible contaminants.

He squatted down next to her, one bare arm held out. "Okay, Doc. Do your worst."

She rose to her knees, moved a bit to take advantage of the slight light nearby where it was slanting through the dense foliage overhead. She'd been right; the bandage was sweat soaked. Loosening the adhesive, she peeled it away, stifling a gasp of pity. The burn was pink and angry looking, still oozing at the edges. She coated the fresh gauze with the medicated ointment and reapplied a fresh bandage. Then she repeated the action for each of his wounds, taking great care to keep her touch gentle.

"I suppose I don't need to ask whether you took any of the pain medication the doctor left you."

He was inspecting her work closely. "Can't afford to. I need to keep my head clear."

"Last time I checked, pain wasn't exactly the best thing for clarity of thinking." When she'd been shot, it had been a toss-up whether she got fuzzier from the prescription pain pills or the agony of the injury itself. But she wasn't going to nag him. She'd stopped the medicine within a couple of days, choosing to suffer the twinges and aches rather than cope with the drowsiness and nausea.

She placed the sterile first-aid supplies back in the Ziploc bag and put it away. Then she dug for a plastic trash bag she had folded up in her pack and withdrew it to shove the wrappers and used bandages in.

He was watching her with a slight smile on his face. "You believe in being prepared."

"Don't you?" Their gazes locked and the smile slowly vanished from his lips.

"Usually." He shifted a little and the width of his shoulders blocked out that single ray of light. "But I gotta admit, I wasn't prepared for you."

Her gaze searched his. There could be several meanings hidden in those words. But what she saw on his face decided the question for her.

Desire.

The recognition had her thoughts splintering. Because she had a strong sense of self-preservation, inner alarms were shrilling like a three-bell fire. There was no basis for a relationship here. She still recalled exactly what the man was capable of.

But thoughts of the future, of what awaited her in the States seemed far away now. Everything around her was so foreign it was difficult to get her bearings. Difficult to concentrate on anything outside this moment.

His shirt was still crumpled in one hand. He wore a

ribbed black tank undershirt that clung to his powerful torso and left most of his shoulders and his arms bare. She'd traced the muscles roped there. Kneaded the well-developed pecs. Felt the length and breadth of him stretched on out on top of her, limb to limb, muscle and sinew against curves.

The jungle seemed to fade away. The danger that they should be focused on intermingled with danger of a far different type. And it beckoned with a wild siren call that was the ultimate temptation.

Ava didn't consider herself a risk taker. But she was teetering on the brink now of a perilous choice. One she'd have trouble forgiving herself for later.

Drawing in a breath, she sat back on her haunches, busying herself tucking things back into her backpack. She could feel him watching her, sensed the control he was trying to exert over his own emotions. "Are we still being smart?"

Her lungs felt strangled. "We have to be."

He muttered an oath she pretended not to hear and then rose. Pulling his shirt back on, he buttoned it before going to his own bag and swiftly replacing things inside. "Bad timing. But this isn't over, Ava." The look he gave her was a searing promise.

Shaken, she stood, slipped her arms back into her pack. Retrieved her rifle. He was right about one thing. This wasn't the time to be distracted by the chemistry that flickered to life whenever they were together.

But she wasn't taking him up on his promise, either. A shudder of disappointment shook her. Despite the fact that they were on the same side for the moment, she hoped she had just enough self-respect left to refrain from sleeping with the man who'd threatened to destroy her.

"I see it."

Adrenaline spiked through him as Ava's quiet voice sounded in the whisper mic.

"How far?"

"Another hour-and-a-half trek, I'd guess."

Thunder rumbled overhead. Any stray rays of light that had been piercing the jungle canopy were gone. With a feeling of resignation, he figured they were lucky they hadn't been rained on before. This far into the mountains, there was bound to be heavy precipitation daily.

"I see four cells."

Hope flickered. That would account for Perez, Reynolds, de la Reyes and Fuente. Maybe they were all alive. But they'd have to be prepared for the possibility that at least one of them would be too badly injured to make it to safety.

Unless he arranged one hell of a diversion for the rebels.

"I've got a visual of Fuente." Ava's voice sounded strained. "No one else I recognize. I'm coming down."

By the time she was on the ground again, Cael had a sheet of paper unrolled from his pack and a marker in his hand. "Draw it out for me."

Ava crouched down beside him, but not, he noted, before checking the ground carefully for anything that crawled or slithered. Taking the marker from him, she began drawing a diagram. "The cells are at the back of the camp, situated similarly to the last location they deserted. Smaller buildings are up and dotted around the area." She drew them in. "A main structure is being constructed in the center. Really, by the time they're done, the whole setup will be a carbon copy of the one they vacated." She made some *X*s around the drawing. "These indicate where I saw guards patrolling."

Cael studied the drawing intently. Six guards for an inner perimeter. Six for outer. They were taking no chances with a high-profile prisoner like the president.

She was looking at him, something in her expression warning him.

"What?"

"I couldn't see who was in the cells. But I could see who *wasn't* in them."

When he frowned, she went on, "Cael, Marissa Fuente was out walking around, chatting with rebel soldiers. She's certainly not wearing the dress she was 'kidnapped' in. And she's looking remarkably at home."

"She was in on it," he said, stunned.

There was no reflection of his surprise in her grim expression. "Bitch. I should have hurt her when I took her down that first night."

Ava had suspected the woman had a hand in it, he recalled. But he was more than a little bemused. Fuente's talents were wasted on the runway. She should have been in Hollywood.

He said as much and Ava snorted. "Men. Big boobs strike you all blind. She played us. Well, she played de la Reyes longer," she amended. "But now we know what really had her cutting her trip short."

"So was she working for Ramirez all along or did he get to her after the assassination attempt failed?" he wondered aloud.

She lifted a shoulder. "Does it matter? She's in this up to her scrawny neck."

He pursed his lips, considering. "Then who's in the fourth cell?" They looked at each other, silent for a moment. As mobile as the camps were, the rebels weren't going to waste time constructing something that wasn't immediately needed. "Maybe she was locked up but, uh…traded some favors for better treatment."

Grimacing, Ava looked back at the map. "Either way, we can't trust her not to sound the alarm when we're getting the others out."

He nodded. The one positive thing was that they could be fairly certain de la Reyes was there if Fuente was.

He tried not to worry about his operatives. If they weren't there, he had another search-and-rescue mission ahead of him. Because he wasn't leaving the country with two of his men unaccounted for.

"It'd be best if you stayed here while I go on ahead to recon." With a sinking feeling, he correctly interpreted the flinty glare she fixed him with. "I need to assess the security and this is outside your area of expertise. It makes sense—"

"It makes sense for you to have someone covering your back when you're entering enemy territory."

He eyed her unblinkingly. "You didn't sign on for this. Think I don't realize that? You're in uncharted waters and I can guarantee you things will deviate from the best plan we come up with. And I have to react to those deviations. It would be best if you could disavow all knowledge of such actions."

Cael expected her temper. He expected an argument. He wasn't prepared for the flash of hurt that flickered across her expression. "Because you think I'll give the information to Samuelson. Help him twist things to hang you." She rose in a lithe, boneless move he couldn't have imitated if he tried. She tried for a careless shrug. Didn't quite pull it off. "You're wise to be cautious, I suppose, given your history."

He felt exceedingly dim-witted. His mind was grappling to connect that flicker of pain he'd seen in her expression with the matter-of-fact tone he heard now. The one that rang false on about a dozen different levels.

"Wait a minute." She strode rapidly ahead of him, just as he felt the first splat of rain on his head. "Dammit, Ava, wait, would you?" He caught up with her as just as the sky opened up in earnest, a torrential downpour that was only minimally blocked by the canopy overhead.

Grabbing her elbow, he halted her, turning her to face him. "You're way off base here."

"Am I?" She gave him a tight smile, yanked at her elbow. He refused to release her. "You told me the same thing last night, remember? You didn't want me along because you couldn't trust me. Not like it's the first time I've heard it."

The temper inside him ignited like a lit fuse. But it wasn't directed at her but himself. "Dammit, will you listen? I don't want any of this touching you! I'm not going to give Samuelson ammunition to be used against you in this. I'm having a hard enough time figuring out a way to keep him away from you once you're back in the States."

"I'd be a fool to believe you."

"Yeah? Well, the joke's on me, sweetheart." The fury was churning in him now. "Because I'm the one who's been the fool all along. I've made excuses for you since the beginning, do you know that? And now when I have Samuelson in my sights, instead of planning for the killing strike, all I can worry about is how to keep you safe from him. I can't afford the luxury of worrying about you. The man's a threat as long as he's in a position of power."

She met him glare for glare, temper for temper. Their argument was none the less fervent for being conducted in near whispers. "Luxury? Who asked for your concern? Not me. I've been taking care of myself since I was fifteen years old. Before that. Forget any plans as they pertain to me. I don't need your protection. Not here. Not when I get back home."

"Don't you think I'd like to forget it?" he said bitterly. "It'd be a helluva lot easier if I could do what's the smartest without considering how it affects you. But I can't." She was staring at him now, the rain pouring over her, forming rivulets to trace down her exquisite features. Frustration pumped through him. "This is a whole new way for me to think, and believe me, I'd give anything to be able to switch it off."

Abruptly he let go of her, and brushed by her to take the lead, almost welcoming the downpour of rain in his face as he strode in the direction of the camp she'd spotted.

Forget about her. He swiped the moisture off his face and plunged ahead. Damned if he didn't wish he could.

* * *

The rain stopped as quickly as it had begun, the clouds parting for the sun to turn the jungle into a vat of steam. The back of Ava's calves ached with exertion. The precipitation had turned the ground into slippery oozy mud. Every step she took the mud seemed to suck at her boot, vacuuming it back to the earth. By the time they'd walked a half mile, the muscles in her legs were trembling like leaves in a windstorm. It was getting more and more difficult even to reach out to hold a large fern or vine out of the way to duck under it.

The bone-deep exhaustion she felt was almost a relief. It made it almost impossible to think about the revelation Cael had made earlier.

Almost.

Her mind skittered uneasily away from his declaration, before creeping up to it again, afraid to examine his meaning too closely. Temper had stripped them both of subterfuge, that was clear. But she still had a difficult time believing concern for her was was the source of his frustration.

She couldn't recall the last time anyone had been worried about her.

When she was growing up, she'd quickly learned that her father had no patience for emotion, so injuries were downplayed. Tears were swallowed. And Danny had always been less focused on the dangers of her job than with the choices she had to make on it, especially as a sniper.

This…this was personal. And she didn't quite know how to deal with it.

Her mental meanderings were halted when Cael threw an arm out to stop her. He had a finger raised to his lips and she understood. They were close to the outer perimeter. Obviously he wasn't leaving anything to chance. He pointed at her, at a tree several yards away and made a crouching movement. He wanted her out of sight. She waited until he finished his signals, understanding that he was going to try to get closer for surveillance.

He got down on his hands and knees and scooped up mud to cover his bare skin. Ava melted back into the trees, choosing a different one to scale than the one he'd indicated. She tucked her rifle into some nearby vegetation. Halfway up the tree she came face-to-face with a revolting spider that was twice as big as her hand.

Fear was a powerful impetus. She fairly flew the rest of the way up. When she got close enough to the top that she could get a view, she rested for a moment, her whole body shaking with distaste and exertion. Then she reached for the binoculars and began scanning.

She was close enough to see the men in the cells, since the structures had no roofs, leaving the prisoners at the mercy of the elements. And all four cells were occupied. She recognized de la Reyes in one. Reynolds in another. She couldn't make out the faces of the other two.

What she could see had her breath strangling in her throat. Cael was inching toward the camp clearing, on his elbows and knees.

And twenty yards from him, a San Baltes rebel soldier stood, rifle raised, pointed right at Cael's head.

Chapter 12

Ava's throat closed. "Rifle twenty yards to your right," she said into the mic, voice strangled.

Even as she spoke the words, he was a blur of motion. She lost sight of him for an instant or two as he rolled, then came to his feet a few feet from the soldier. Everything slowed to still frames. The rifle barrel swinging to follow him. Cael's arm pulling back. Then shooting forward. A blade she hadn't even seen him holding whirling through the air, striking the soldier. Burying to the hilt itself in his heart.

As she watched, the soldier swayed, began to crumple. Cael caught him before he hit the ground, then dragged him deeper into the jungle. He came out alone a moment later. Commenced his recon as if nothing had happened.

Ava didn't recover nearly so quickly. Reaction set in, a giant shudder working over her body. Dropping the glasses for a moment, she just rested her forehead against the limb and waited for the shaking to stop.

He could have been killed. The body amid the fronds and ferns could have been his. It was going to take a while to recover from that knowledge. And the response it was wreaking in her system.

But then, shoulders squaring, she took up position again. Because there was only so much surveillance that could be accomplished on the ground. Aerial intel was her specialty.

And it just might be the only thing that would save Cael from the next soldier who happened by.

She scanned the area carefully, pausing on the scene taking place in the middle of the compound. The man standing in the center seemed to be shouting at two of his soldiers. Frowning, she adjusted her glasses to get a closer look. The two men seemed to be protesting or explaining something. In the next moment the man in charge pulled out a handgun.

The sound of the shots could be heard faintly in the distance. First one body crumpled. Then another. The officer—because clearly this person appeared in charge of the rebels—gestured to another couple of soldiers, who moved rapidly to do his bidding.

Ava held her breath. Because this time the soldiers were heading toward the cells.

She looked for Cael. Had difficulty finding him. If she hadn't been searching for him she never would have spotted him wearing that lightweight gillie suit. As if was, after straining for several moments she spotted him a hundred meters to the right of where he'd encountered the first soldier.

"Guard at left, twenty meters," she breathed into the whisper mic. She figured he saw him. But why he was maintaining that proximity rather than doing recon from farther out she couldn't guess. But she was beginning to believe the man did everything the hard way.

She switched her attention back on the events in the camp. One of the prisoners had been dragged across the compound and was on his knees in front of the officer, who was beating him with the butt of a rifle.

De la Reyes.

Ava released the glasses and picked up her rifle. Sighted. Nerves clutched in her stomach. Because there was no commander making the decisions from a nearby command post. No one issuing the weapons tight or weapons loose command. She didn't dare another communication to Cael as close as he was to that soldier. She'd have to make the split-second decision herself.

But what would be the right decision to make? Saving de la Reyes by shooting the officer would alert the camp and endanger the other prisoners, making a rescue attempt likely unsuccessful.

In the end, it was a decision she wasn't faced with. At least not yet. After beating the president unmercifully, the officer kicked hard at his prone body and had him dragged back to his cell. Ava's throat was tight. De la Reyes appeared unconscious. But he was still alive. And for now, that was going to have to do.

Her muscles were tight with tension. She slid the safety back on her rifle and exchanged it for the high-powered glasses again. Fuente wasn't anywhere in sight. And no matter how hard she scanned the proximity, she couldn't pick up Cael's location. She assumed he'd be making a huge circle well outside the outer perimeter of the compound. And because of the risk of detection, his progress would be slow.

Ava settled herself more comfortably in the notch of the tree and prepared to wait.

"Reynolds was right," Cael reported tersely as they made their way swiftly away from the camp several hours later. "Any infusion of cash they've received from Ramirez has gone into weaponry. For a ragtag bunch of rebels they're packing state-of-the-art rifles. No reason not to believe they've got even more gadgets stored in their artillery shed."

"That must be the structure on the front left of the camp," Ava said. She was moving like an automatom. She'd long since passed the point of simple exhaustion. Her entire body ached from perching in that tree for so long. Her pack seemed to have taken on an additional twenty pounds. And now her boots each seemed to weigh a ton as she slogged through the slick mud of the jungle floor. "I saw a soldier go into it and exchange a rifle for the officer or captain or whoever is in charge." She hesitated a moment over the memory. It had been after the man had violently beaten de la Reyes.

"That's what I figure, too. That's par for the course with an outfit like this. They'll spend the money on weaponry, but they aren't going to use it to update their countersurveillance methods. They're more concerned with keeping the prisoners in than with keeping people out. And that's good news for us."

"I spotted at least three trip wires." She hadn't asked where they were headed. She hoped, *prayed,* it was back to a spot where they could summon the military and then rest safely waiting for reinforcements.

He turned and cocked a brow at her. "Good eyes," he murmured. The admiration in his tone had warmth flickering, proving that everything inside her wasn't numb. The involuntary response made her impatient with herself. Because of him she'd had to learn to pee in a tree. That wasn't a skill she'd ever wanted or needed to acquire before now.

"Actually I found a total of six, all of which I dismantled, and about a dozen booby traps. Strictly low tech. Sentries posted at each of the cells. A half dozen others staggered around the perimeter. Makes it a challenging extraction, but not impossible."

"I spotted de la Reyes being beaten," she said. The image flickered across her mind again, but she firmly pushed it away. It was dangerous to have a connection to one of the parties inside. Made it difficult to maintain the objectivity needed to make sound decisions. "He's not in very good shape."

"I saw it, too." His voice was grim. "Figured maybe those two soldiers that got shot had been posted sentry at his cell. Their infraction might have been minor. Absolute obedience is demanded in these types of camps. Maybe they were heard talking to de la Reyes. Maybe they accepted something from him. Hard to say."

Whatever they'd done had cost them their lives. And had earned the president a serious beating.

Cael stopped to readjust the weight of the pack he was carrying before forging ahead again. "They're savages. Remember that. The rules are different here. The only laws governing these people are those imposed by their leader, who sells their services to the highest bidder. Right now it happens to be Ramirez. But when the past president was in power, this same group made it a habit to kidnap and ransom family members of government officials, often women and children. Fewer than forty percent were returned alive."

A small lizard skittered over the toe of Ava's boot. It was a measure of her exhaustion that she gave it only a glance before kicking it aside with her other foot.

"The soldiers probably won't have had any special training, but you can bet their commander has been trained by PSB Chinese Intel or former SpetzNatz. He'll be one to be careful of. Take him out of the equation and we'll have neutralized the brains of the outfit."

"What happens when the guards' shift changes and the soldier you took out is missed?"

"The shift already changed," he reminded her. "I figure they're rotating on three shifts of eight hours. I'd feel better if I could be sure, though. But unless someone stumbles over his body we'll be okay. Desertion is a constant problem with these groups. The life is hard. They'll likely chalk up his disappearance to that."

But her attention had splintered. She recognized the place they were heading toward. She'd longed to stop there only hours earlier. "Water," she breathed reverently. She could hear it again, the sound of a creek running fast nearby. The thought of cupping her hands in it, dribbling it over her face beckoned like a mirage in a desert.

"Yeah. We need rest. And food. And I have to communicate with Quintero about military intervention."

The rest sounded inviting. So did the thought of food. But nothing could compare with the lure of the water itself. Ava could barely contain herself while they climbed up increasingly steep inclines, which made the muscles in her calves weep. She had a focus now. Something to push through the tiredness for.

But fifteen minutes later when she caught her first sight of the water, she stood, transfixed. She'd hoped for a small stream. Perhaps even deep enough to bathe in. But she'd never expected the beauty she was faced with now.

The water tumbled over a rocky wall perhaps ten feet overhead and pooled between twin towering boulders before continuing in a stream that grew increasing narrow as it continued to the east. Stray rays of sunlight sent rainbows dancing across it as it cascaded into a narrow pool.

"Please tell me there are no piranhas or snakes or anything else creepy to worry about in there."

"Probably not deep enough for piranhas." It didn't escape her that he hadn't addressed the rest of her concern. "But just to be on the safe side, you should probably content yourself with a shower rather than a bath."

She paused impatiently as he stopped and examined the area with his set of high-powered binoculars for five minutes. Ten. Fifteen. Finally, when she was ready to give him a push back down the steep slope they'd climbed, he moved forward. "It looks clear. No reason for the rebels to come this far east for water. They had a lagoon several yards to the south of the camp."

She pushed him to the side and took the lead, stumbling over the roots and rocks that thrust across the jungle floor.

"Okay, you're filthy, I know that. But I'm still calling dibs on the first shower." Fairness went by the wayside after tromping through a tropical jungle for hours. She rationalized that he was probably used to it, so the mud he'd slathered on his body could wait another fifteen minutes to be cleaned off. Or twenty. "I promise not to use up all the hot water."

Ava reached a hand forward and caught a drizzle from the falls in her palm, nearly swooning with delight. She took off the glasses still hanging from a strap around her neck. Shrugged out of the strap holding her rifle, and carefully set it nearby on a pile of stones. Then gracelessly, she let her pack slide off her back and unzipped it, digging around in it for the fresh set of clothes she'd brought.

"The most important thing to remember is fresh socks. Dry your feet thoroughly before putting them on," Cael cautioned. He'd stopped, too, letting his pack slide to the ground, although he retained his rifle. "Check your boots before dressing again in case an unwelcome guest takes up residency in one."

But even as she was stripping off her long-sleeve shirt, enjoying the air on her shoulders, left bare by the stretch camisole, a little sliver of guilt was niggling through her. "On second thought, why don't you go first?"

He looked up, surprised. "First time a woman's ever suggested I use the bathroom first."

And the fact that he'd obviously had plenty of experience in that department almost made her reconsider her offer. "I'll use extra Ziploc bags to cover your wounds. Then we'll need to change the bandages again."

Cael looked amused. "I don't need a nurse. But I appreciate the thought."

He should appreciate it. He had no idea what the offer had cost her. "C'mon. The sooner you get in, the quicker it will be my turn."

Ignoring his continued protests, she stooped to retrieve the first-aid bag she'd brought. It took a bit longer to find the spare plastic bags she'd tucked away amid the food and equipment. One thing her experience camping had taught her was that Ziplocs and rubber bands came in handy at least as often as any other piece of regular camping gear.

Her fingers closed around the plastic and she withdrew what she needed. Then she rose, with the spare plastic bags and tape, and turned to Cael.

Her breath abruptly strangled in her lungs.

He was stripping off the gillie suit, carefully rolling the pieces up and inserting them in his pack. For someone supposedly reluctant to go first, he wasn't wasting a lot of time demurring. His undershirt went next and his chest looked as rock hewn as the boulders near the water. She remembered in intimate detail what it felt like under her fingertips.

Her earlier exhaustion drained away. Nerve endings felt unbearably alive and alert. She became aware of the constant background noise. The gurgling of the water. The chittering of the insects. The squawk of the colorful birds. The jibbering screech of the gibbons and monkeys.

The scene was primitive. Elemental. They were the foreigners in this environment. The jungle life would continue unmarred when they were gone, as if they'd never been here at all. It was dangerously tempting to think anything that happened here occurred without the promise of consequences and regrets.

"Ready?" He was holding out his arms for her to cover the bandages. No wonder he hadn't protested too loudly at the thought of going first. Mud was still caked on his face, neck and hands. The suit had to have acted like a internal oven, elevating his body temperature to unbearable degrees.

Ava swiftly wrapped the plastic bags over the bandages over his arms, securing them in several places with rubber bands.

"I'm not fussy," he said meaningfully, looking at her with an expression she didn't trust. "There's plenty of water for two showering at a time."

Under no circumstances was she going to let him know that she'd noticed that herself. "Maybe *I'm* fussy," she said tartly. And obviously too easily tempted. She ducked around him and grabbed her weapon, strode several yards in the opposite direction, taking great care to keep her gaze from returning to him.

But in the absence of the visual image, her other senses seemed unbearably heightened. She could hear the heavy thud of his boots dropping to the soft ground. The scrape of his zipper sounded, and she knew he was stripping off his pants. Several moments passed before she heard a different pattern of the water hitting the heavy stones. And she knew he was stepping onto the rocks. That he was now standing nude and powerful below the spray.

Ava gritted her teeth, willed her concentration off the man a few yards away and on to any foreign sounds that didn't belong there. But it was difficult to keep her eyes moving over the terrain, yet skirting the one area they most wanted to stray.

She'd done harder things, hadn't she? Held position on assignment for hours while the negotiators tried to talk a hostage taker out. Done overnight surveillance in beat-up cars in front of the apartment of whatever drug dealer they happened to be tailing. Boredom was the enemy on those assignments. Keeping senses sharp for that split second when everything could change.

And she needed sharp senses here, too. In case he'd been wrong about anyone else coming here.

But as the minutes ticked by, no sound marred the drone of the insects. Nothing was heard that didn't belong in the jungle chorus. And her nerves stretched and tightened taut as piano wire. Her blood began to throb with a primal sort of beat in keeping with the elemental setting.

A twig snapped behind her and she spun, bringing up the rifle and sighting with one smooth motion. The large wild pig that had started for the stream froze, stared back at her. In the next instant it turned and plunged back into the jungle with surprising speed.

Even as she lowered her rifle her gaze went helplessly to the man standing under the water. Found him watching her. He made no attempt to hide his stirring interest, and the sight of his masculinity weakened her earlier resolve.

It was a moment out of time. As if the rest of the world spun on its axis, leaving this place, this minute untouched. And if the world couldn't intrude on this space, neither could the worries that followed it.

He held a hand out to her then, a silent entreaty she knew better than to accept. But her feet were moving of their own volition, her gaze never leaving his.

He'd slicked his wet hair back with careless fingers and his pale green eyes were alight with a hunger that staggered her. She fumbled a little with the rifle, resecuring the safety and setting it aside.

The task of unlacing her boots should have given her several moments to come to her senses. Would have, if he didn't present a carnal picture of arousal. To have that searing intensity focused on her was its own sort of temptation. One she was no longer interested in battling.

She couldn't remember the last time she'd stripped for a man. The act was less seduction than functionality. She wanted to be as naked as he was. Wanted, finally, to feel every inch of his slick skin pressed against hers.

The dark fatigues were removed next. A muscle jumped in his clenched jaw and she enjoyed his reaction enough to slow her movements. Make them more deliberate. If this was to be a stolen moment, it should be one worth remembering. The urgency drawn painfully tight inside her loosened a notch.

So she drew out the task of removing her top. Hooked her fingers beneath the hem to bare one inch of flesh at a time. Watched his gaze scorch her with a primitive hunger she didn't remember ever eliciting from a man before. It made her feel exquisitely attractive, heady with feminine power.

It was too easy to feel at one in the primitive setting. To

feel as basic and elemental as the wildness around them. Especially with this wild pagan tattoo beat in her pulse.

Cael's face could have been chiseled from the stone he stood upon. But his eyes were alight with a savage promise that sent little spirals of thrill up her spine. And when she dropped her top to the pile of her clothes, the leap of desire in his expression turned her muscles to warm wax.

One arm snaked out, still wrapped in plastic, and took her hand, tugging. She swayed, trying to retain her balance, but landed right where he'd intended, in his arms.

The water spraying over them was colder than she'd expected. But it couldn't come close to cooling the heat that seemed to scorch her from the inside out. When he set her on her feet, she stepped closer and snaked her arms around his neck, her lips going in search of his mouth.

Their kiss rocked her off balance for a moment, and she clung to him even more tightly to right herself. His kiss was a demand she fully reciprocated. His mouth crushed down over hers, as if something wild had been unleashed. Something she welcomed. Something she returned.

Their lips mated, twisting together, tongues and teeth clashing in a tangle of need. The taste of him was hot and wild. Addictive and intoxicating. It sped to her veins and turned her blood molten.

Desperate need fueled them. As if each was anxious to forget all the reasons they'd denied themselves this. All the reasons it would never happen again. Ava was dimly aware they should slow down. Savor every brush of skin. Every sigh.

But there was no slowing with lightning jumping and flashing to life between them. No thought of drawing this out, one delicious moment at a time when sensations bumped and collided with each glide of a tongue. With each deliberate stroke.

His hands streaked over her, leaving liquid fire in their wake. She was just as greedy in her need for the feel of flesh.

Her palms swept up his sides on a rollicking exploration. There was pleasure in testing the firm pecs. The heavy shoulders, with their sculpted muscle. The strong, bulging arms. The hair-roughened chest. The flat, firm abdomen. Stopping to caress the hard straining length of him, thick and engorged.

She wasn't a woman who indulged in pretense or coyness. With something so important to hide in her life, it seemed imperative to be up-front in all her other dealings. Sex was a simple, natural act, and if it was one she hadn't bothered to indulge in recently, that was by choice. It was easy to turn away from the urge when it didn't rage like a fire through her system, a burning demand for release.

She tore her mouth from his, took a deep breath. And lost it in the next moment when he cupped her breasts in his hands, fingers teasing her nipples. Leaning forward, she dragged her sensitive lips over the stubble on his jaw, enjoying the slight abrasion. Her fingers traced the triangular patch of hair across his chest, to where it narrowed to a thin trail on his belly, then skated to his sides, exploring the smooth skin stretched over muscle.

His mouth lowered then and took one nipple in his mouth, his tongue lashing it before he suckled her strongly. Colors wheeled beneath her closed eyelids, sensation bursting forth in a tidal wave of need.

Ava arched her back, exulting in the freedom afforded by raw unvarnished passion. There was no room for pretense here, no deception. He touched her like he was staking a claim, as if he sought to brand himself on her memory.

She felt him drawing her panties down her legs and he raised his head long enough to rasp, "Step out of them." She obeyed, even as she took his heavy masculinity between her palms and lingered to caress.

Cael's breath hissed in and his eyes slitted closed and she tortured him with long, slow strokes, fingers tightening in a motion meant to drive him just a little mad. She enjoyed watching him as passion worked over him. Enjoyed seeing hunger stamp itself on his tough warrior exterior. He looked no less savage lost in passion. And she exulted in that, too, the image releasing fireballs of lust through her veins.

He was no different in need than he was in battle, she thought dimly, as his hand slid up her thigh, cupped her feminine mound. Tough, aggressive and slightly ruthless. She didn't know what that said about her to find the combination so arousing.

She traced his collarbone with her lips, exploring the intriguing hollow where sinew met bone. There was pleasure to be had in just looking at him, broad and hard, with faded scars scattered over his chest. His mouth left her breast and she felt his lips on the still pink and puckered scar above her left breast. Knew he'd recognize it as a gunshot wound. Would acknowledge it without the fascinated horror most would react with.

And in that way they were alike. Their lives, their choices on the job put them in danger, which was accepted rather than feared.

Then conscious thought deserted her as his touch grew more intimate. His voice in her ear was ragged, and the evidence of his fraying control would have been exhilarating if hers hadn't fragmented already.

"You're like wet silk here." His fingers parted her folds, rubbed against the taut bundle of nerves hidden there. "And here." One finger stroked inside her, and Ava gave a little cry as her knees went to water. "Tight and hot." His forehead rested against hers even as his arm tightened around here, taking more of her weight. "I want to be inside you. But not before I see you come apart for me." He probed more deeply, while his thumb rubbed rhythmically at her clitoris.

Every teasing stroke sent sensation arrowing to her womb and desperation clutched there, mingled with desire. She wanted him with her, every inch of the sensual journey. Wanted to see him staggered and shattered, as defenseless as she against the sensual assault.

Her touch became less teasing than demanding, and a part of her thrilled at the low groan coming from his throat. But in the next moment he drew her hands away from him with his free hand, keeping them clasped easily.

A surge of frustration pierced her. "You don't play fair," she gasped.

"Just evening the playing field," he muttered, his mouth stringing a line of stinging kisses up her jaw. "There's been nothing *fair* about my reaction to you from the beginning. You make me crazy." He drew her earlobe between his teeth, worried it gently. "I'm just returning the favor."

She twisted ineffectually against him in an attempt to free her hands, moaned when the motion embedded his finger even more deeply. His touch grew more deliberate, his thumb tapping at the tight bundle of nerves between her thighs. And when he took a nipple between his teeth, scraped it intentionally, sensation rose up and slammed against sensation, catapulting her to a bone-shattering release.

Long moments later she became aware of the band of steel at her back where his arm braced her. Still dazed and trembling, she slid her freed hands around his neck as he withdrew his touch. Shudders were racking his powerful body like a stallion on the scent. She dragged her lips across his mouth even as she felt him lifting her.

Legs folding around his waist, Ava dragged her eyes open, fighting off the stupor of satisfaction to watch him. Her pulse stuttered to life again. His face was flushed with arousal, the skin pulled tightly across his cheekbones. And his eyes…the heat there sent little flickers of answering flame licking through her veins again.

The water coursed over them, leaving tiny streams on his cheeks, which could have been carved from granite. She was half surprised when it didn't leave a trail of steam in its wake. And when she lowered a hand to touch his manhood again, it strained to her touch.

She shifted in his arms, guiding him to her softness, intent on drawing it out. But Cael grasped her hips in frantic hands and surged upward, seating himself fully inside her with one desperate stroke.

Impossibly, the fire began again in her blood, in her pulse. He was all she was aware of, this man and each individual sensation he elicited. Desire, so recently satiated, leapt forward like an uncaged tiger. Ava wrapped her arms around his shoulders, her lips searching for his as he began to thrust within her.

Heels digging into his hips, she joined him in a race toward satisfaction. Sensation collided with sensation. The water pouring over them, doing little to cool their fevered flesh. The slickness of their skin as their bodies pressed together. The wild pounding in her blood that threatened to erupt with every deep thrust.

Their bodies strained together, each movement aimed at getting closer, deeper. And she felt a clutch of satisfaction when she saw his face as he crested. His fingers grasped her hips more desperately and he pounded into her as the madness took him. And when she heard his ragged groan, heard her name on his lips, the sound triggered her own release and she followed him headlong into pleasure.

Chapter 13

At Cael's suggestion they didn't fully dress while they rested. And it was much more comfortable to sit on the bedding he'd constructed of cut ferns with the gillie suit on top, dressed only in a tank and fresh underwear.

It also felt a bit decadent to lie there against his bare chest in the dim sunlight of the jungle around them, feeling at one with the primitive surroundings.

Cael was propped up against the pile of boulders with one arm around her waist, keeping her close to him. Ava had never been a cuddler. And sex this mind shattering left her feeling exposed and vulnerable, scrambling for defenses. But they were difficult to summon with her head lying on his chest. Listening to the strong thud of his heart beating in her ear. The position was too intimate. Too tempting to believe there was more between them than the act that had left them shaking and breathless.

His breathing was deep and even. He was silent so long she

thought he slept. But then he spoke, and his words had ice abruptly forming in her veins. "I've seen your father on TV. Heard bits of some of his speeches. You're nothing like him."

Tension shot into her muscles. She stiffened, meaning to move away, but his arm kept her close.

"Not for lack of trying on his part. He raised me, or tried to, in his own image." And that's what had the shame rearing its ugly head. Recalling how she'd made the posters. Typed the speeches he'd dictated. Accepted as truth the hatred he'd spewed with little question.

"So he's always held those views?"

"Always." She thought, she hoped, that her terse answer would stem any more questions. His next words proved her wrong.

"You said once he'd taught you to shoot."

"We were living on a white supremacy compound in Montana," she recalled quietly. Surrounded by people who shared the same beliefs. Espoused the same views. "We used to have competitions. As I got better he started enrolling me in contests all over the state." It was the most normal memory she had of her childhood. Striving to improve in the one area in which she could impress her father. Winning, if not his love, at least a measure of respect.

"When I was in eighth grade I started riding a bus to public school." It was then, she recalled, that she first started experiencing questions about all she'd learned from her father. For the first time she began forming some of her own opinions. And she'd paid, dearly, every time she dared utter them at home. He'd once given her a black eye for daring to disagree with him about biracial dating. "I started seeing him differently. Questioning his views. He didn't like that. And when I got pregnant at fifteen he beat me so badly I almost lost the baby. Then he threw me out. I haven't seen him since."

Every muscle in his body seemed to tense. "He deserted you?"

"I'm lucky he didn't kill me. Alex's father is Hispanic."

And Eduardo had been the first human being in her life to offer her love, or what she'd interpreted as such. From the distance of age she could see now how panicked he was when she'd told him. How afraid for his own future. At the time she only felt deserted and betrayed.

And completely alone.

His voice sounded strained. "How did you manage?"

"A guidance counselor helped get me placed in a foster family. Assisted in getting services for me and the baby." And it was through going to church with the foster family that she'd met Danny. Two years later they were married and moving to California where he was going to seminary.

As always the ancient history left her feeling depressed. "I'm not proud of the fact that I spent two years trying to get my father to see me. Even convinced myself he'd want to have a relationship with Alex, since he was a boy. I should have known better." And what a narrow miss that had been, she thought with an inner shudder. How horrible it would have been for Alex to have been exposed to the same sort of intolerance she'd been raised with. To have been made to feel that he was somehow less simply because of the color of his skin.

"It worked out for the best." At least she'd always thought so. Had often congratulated herself on how she'd kept the Julson name from ever tainting her son. Her career. Her life.

Until now.

Earlier thoughts of the future had seemed distant and foreign. Now the worry crowded in again, insistent and troubling. She tried to sit up, to edge away. Cael kept her firmly in place.

"I won't use him against you," he said quietly. "Your father. After what I imagine you went through with him, I could never do that to you. But I still believe Samuelson will. And I've had a couple ideas, but still don't have anything foolproof planned that will protect you from him."

Lead coated the bottom of her stomach, and a feeling of resignation filled her. "I know. I called Alex before I left." And he'd been angry, vehemently so, when she confessed she'd lied to him all these years. But even in the face of his fury, the disappointment in her that he hadn't tried to mask, she hadn't disclosed her father's name. She needed to be there with him for that. Ava couldn't stand the thought of her son researching Calvin Julson on his own and discovering what the man was. "I'll tell him everything when I get back. He's furious with me right now. I hope he'll come to understand. He's pretty great."

"I'm not surprised. His mother is rather outstanding herself."

Ridiculous to feel this warm glow at his words. Ridiculous when so much between them was tenuous and built on misunderstanding and distrust. Because she didn't know how to respond to his words, was afraid to read too much into them, she continued. "Alex made it easy. He hasn't ever been much of a problem. He's scary smart. Athletic." She gave a little laugh thinking of their last argument before she'd left. "The biggest problem he gives me is getting all weird about being seen in public with me. He has a fit about going to the mall. Something about his friends calling me a MILF. I figure that's probably some derogatory teen slang for cop or something."

When Cael made a choking sound, she turned in his arms to look up at him inquiringly. "What? Do you know what it means?"

"I do. And it most definitely doesn't have anything to do with your occupation. At least not with the department."

She didn't trust that light in his eyes any more than she did the humor in his voice. "What's it mean, then?"

He ducked his head to drop a kiss under her ear. "MILF, my naive Ava, stands for Mothers I'd Like to…" The last word was whispered in her ear, and had her jerking upward in indignation.

"You're making that up!"

"I most definitely am not. I believe the term was coined in a movie, one starring a bunch of horny teenaged boys."

Fuming, she gave in to the gentle pressure he was exerting

to get her to relax against him again. "The little jerks. If I ever hear one of them saying it, I'll slap cuffs on him and throw him in juvie."

Laughter sounded in his voice. "Just more fodder for an adolescent boy's porn-filled fantasies, but hey, whatever works."

She reached behind her and grabbed a tuft of chest hair, gave it a tug, satisfied when he gave a quiet yelp. "Your whole gender is seriously depraved. Maybe I should lock my son up before he gets corrupted by it."

"Believe me, if he's...what? Fifteen? He's corrupted already."

She didn't share his amusement. What mother wanted to think about her son's development into a man? Although she had the sneaking thought that if Alex grew up with a few of Cael McCabe's qualities, he'd be quite a man indeed.

"Better try to get some rest." He stroked a hand down her back. "We'll take turns."

"I can take first watch," she objected even as heaviness began creeping into her limbs.

"I need to finalize the plans for the rescue." As if in recognition of the questions on her lips, he soothed her. "Go to sleep. We can talk about them later."

It was a measure of her exhaustion that she put aside the nerves and uncertainty about the night ahead. She felt herself sliding down the slippery slope toward sleep. Dreamless except for a green-eyed man who was ruthless and tender by turn.

Although the sun hadn't completely slipped behind the mountains, the jungle was already shadowy with the approach of night. "We need to discuss this further."

Cael finished donning the gillie suit and bent to inspect his pack. "There's nothing to discuss."

Ava stared at the back of him, her teeth grinding with frustration. "We could start with this idea of yours. And your totally incomprehensible refusal to use the military for assistance."

"We can't trust them." His voice was the measured one an adult used with a child who refused to take no for an answer. And made her want to smack him for it. "We don't know who all Ramirez has gotten to. We can't afford chancing that someone will tip him off about the raid tonight. We'd be walking into a trap then."

"So it's a risk." With furious movements she finished dressing, any lingering softness she'd felt as he'd slept with his head in her lap long since gone. "It's also a risk to depend on Reynolds and Perez being in good enough shape to help you once you release them. Hell, you'll probably be killed trying to get to them. Not to mention how you figure on getting out with all the hostages."

"I've explained the plan. It has a fair chance for success. The military should be standing by, per Quintero's orders. When everyone is safely released we'll arrange a diversion and radio for help. Chopper should be here in fifteen, twenty minutes."

Every time he mentioned the plan her veins filled with ice. "That can be a lifetime when we're being chased by over a hundred soldiers!"

He rose, shot her a feral grin. "Well, I'm gonna try to make sure most of them are otherwise occupied."

"It's too risky," she said stubbornly. The thought of him sneaking into the camp, alone, had panic slicking down her spine.

His expression sobered. "If you can't do this, you need to tell me now. I'll have to think of another way. But I still won't alert the military until it's too late for the commander of that camp to get tipped off."

She stared at him in frustration. It was like trying to reason with a slab of granite. Her logic bounced ineffectually off him. And she didn't like walking into any assignment with this fear circling frantically in her belly. Fear for him.

"If things look impossible we'll abort," he said, his voice muffled as he squatted to the ground and started rubbing mud on his face. "And if things go FUBAR, you know what to do."

The nausea that rose at the thought nearly choked her. Fade back into the jungle. Make her way to safety and radio Quintero with the coordinates to chance a military rescue.

Leave McCabe's body where it fell.

Just the thought was very nearly paralyzing. He thought she was considering the risk to herself. Ava didn't bother to inform him the thought of him dying in the attempt was closing her throat with fear. It was impossible to consider how she could feel so deeply for the man when she hadn't even known him two weeks ago. When the majority of their relationship had consisted in subterfuge and deception.

She watched him numbly as he made his preparations, trying to calm the nerves jumping and skittering inside her. She was of no use to him with this kind of emotion roiling inside her. Her experience on SWAT had taught her that. If she couldn't reach for calm, she could endanger him with an overreaction. She could get him killed.

He crossed to her then, and scooped up more mud, rubbed it gently across her cheeks. "Seems a shame to cover up this face," he said huskily.

She swallowed hard, her hands coming up to clasp around his wrists, stopping him. "McCabe."

Stilling, he surveyed her somberly. She drew a deep breath. Let it out in a slow stream. "If you get killed tonight, you are seriously going to piss me off."

His mouth kicked up in a one-sided grin and he leaned in for a hard, thorough kiss. When he lifted his mouth, he said huskily, "I know how dangerous your temper is. So I'm going to do my best to stay on your good side."

They moved silently through the darkened jungle. Cael looked over his shoulder to check on Ava's progress, found her close behind him. And probably still not thrilled with the plan he'd come up with. But he'd come equipped for the type of rescue he had planned. Not Hollywood's idea, of course, with mercs carrying clanking ammo belts and Uzis strapped across their chests. But for a silent deadly entry into the camp and hopefully an unnoticed escape, the idea was fast, silent and deadly.

He halted and handed her a single-bladed knife, keeping the larger, more deadly blade for himself. She took it without comment and slipped it into her belt.

"We can't risk using the wrist communicators from here on in," he cautioned her in a barely audible whisper. He could barely make out her features, darkened as they were with the mud he'd rubbed on them. He knew he looked just as alien with his face blackened and fading into the hood of his gillie suit. "Only shoot if it becomes absolutely necessary. I know you've got a flash and sound suppressor, but we don't want to take any chances."

"You mean because you're already taking such a huge risk yourself?" she muttered.

He was smart enough to ignore her. "You take up position here. You're behind and in the center of the three guards who have the best view of the cells from the perimeter. I'll take care of them before going in." And anyone else who happened to notice him and tried to sound an alarm.

"What are you going to do if Reynolds and Perez are in no shape to help once you get them out?" she demanded in a furious whisper. "Unless you're planning to don a red cape and tights, I don't think you're capable of hauling three prisoners out on your back with no one being the wiser."

"Let me cross that bridge when I come to it," he responded evenly. But he knew it wasn't a matter of *if* something went wrong on these assignments but *when*. And he questioned himself whether he could maintain the objectivity needed to abort if necessary, leaving his client and friends to the mercy of the rebels.

"Just be sure to stay down and out of sight." He studied her in the darkness, most of the words he wanted to utter remaining unspoken. Hell of a thing for a man to finally figure out what he needed saying at the worst possible moment. "We've got some things to iron out when this is over."

"When this is over I'm still going to be harboring a serious grudge over this whole mess," she said. "It's going to take some pretty smooth talking on your part."

Something lightened inside him as he fixed the night-vision goggles over his eyes. "Smooth's my middle name."

The first sentry was sloppy. Propped against the trunk of a tree, he was lighting a cigarette when Cael took him out. He dragged his body a little ways away and divested the man of his rifle and ammo. Then he belly-crawled to the next sentry, one excruciating inch at a time. This one was more alert. More of a challenge. When Cael finally reached him and rose, the man, seeming to sense his presence, started to turn, his rifle raised.

Cael sprang then, the wire in his hands held tight. Their battle was short, vicious and in the end, one-sided. When the guard's body went limp beneath him he started to rise. Heard a sound not much louder than a polite cough.

His focus snapped toward the direction of the third guard in time to see him jerk midstride in his race in this direction. Watched him drop to the ground, lie motionless.

The first thing to go wrong tonight almost had. Chalk one up for Ava.

He disposed of the bodies and collected the weapons. Dropping to his belly, he crawled a few yards and stashed them in some brush, hoping he got a chance to come back for them. Then he took several minutes to get a look at what was going on down below.

Two guards were on duty outside the cells. Neither man gave any indication that he'd noticed anything untoward a hundred meters from the camp. This was where the plan got a bit dicier.

Cael had a moment to hope that Ava was keeping an eye on the guard on the northeast corner of the perimeter. If the man moved to just the right position at exactly the right time, he might get a glimpse of something going on in the camp.

Cael had to move faster than caution dictated. He couldn't afford to wait long enough for a shift change. The perimeter guards would notice when three of the soldiers they went to replace were gone.

Close enough now to hear the occasional murmurs of the sentries standing guard over the cells. He couldn't catch their words, but their tones were relaxed.

The first cell held de la Reyes. After the beating he'd taken that day, he'd need assistance getting out of here. Cael bypassed the cell and moved stealthily to the next. Scooping up some of the mud beneath him, he rolled it into little balls and tossed one against the side of the first cell hoping to draw a guard's attention. Then he waited, muscles alert to an almost painful pitch.

But nothing happened.

Swearing silently, he deliberately scuffed a heel on one of the wooden slats on the back of Reynolds's cell. Heard the guards' low conversation stop. He saw one rise, round the first cell to check out the noise.

Knife in hand, Cael was waiting for him. The silent attack was swift and deadly. Holding the man's limp body in front of him, he waited quietly for the second guard to come looking for the man when he didn't return.

"Que usted esta haciendo? Tomar un escape?"

The other sentry's low whisper sounded after several minutes.

Cael waited, barely breathing. A shadow moved across the slats of the cell he leaned against. If Reynolds were in decent shape, he'd be alert to what was transpiring outside his prison. He'd be ready to move at a moment's notice.

Cael could hear the other guard's approach. Cautious. He'd be wary now, since his colleague hadn't answered. The trick was keeping him from sounding an alarm before Cael could disarm him.

He drew farther into the space between the first two cells. Leaned the guard's dead body against the first structure. Waited for the footsteps to round the corner. Cael backed up stealthily and took a quick look at the area in front of the cells. Deserted.

With one arm he extended his rifle while backing around the front of the president's cell. Listened for the guard to approach stealthily. He gave the body a jab with his rifle and it fell at the second guard's feet even as he dodged around the first cell.

He was behind the second guard even as he crouched to catch his colleague. With a flash of his knife, he dispatched him as quickly as he had the first one.

Dragging both bodies to the far side of de la Reyes's cell, he let them lie there before going to Reynolds's cell, keeping a wary watch on any undue activity in the camp. His face close against the slats of the second cell, he whispered, "Kill zone."

There was a moment of silence. Then a barely audible reply. "Hell box."

Cael knew better then to reveal his location with a flash of teeth, but he grinned inwardly, relief washing over him. It was Reynolds inside all right. The code was derived from their first experience after BUDS training, arranging ambushes for guerilla rebels.

Staying low, he reached up and unlatched the cord holding the cell door shut. Reynolds came out low, and the two of them squatted in between the first two cells. Cael handed him the extra rifle he'd taken off the first perimeter sentry he'd taken out. "What's the lowdown?"

"Fuente's in on it."

Ava had already called that. She'd suspected as much from the beginning.

"The rebel captain sent a small squad out late this afternoon to take the bitch back to town. Probably to get her reward from Ramirez. He executed two guards today who were on duty last night. Accused them of giving de la Reyes preferential treatment."

"I saw it."

"The squad is supposed to come back with word from Ramirez about something they want de la Reyes to do." Reynolds was already picking up the soft mud from the ground and rubbing it on his hands and face.

"Unfreeze Ramirez's assets."

"If it's done, he'll be a dead man."

"Not if we get him out of here first. Is Perez here?"

"In the cell at the far end. I don't know who's on the other side of me, but I know he's an American."

They'd take him with them when they left. And it was high time for them to leave. Cael dug into his pack, withdrew two grenades. He handed one to the other man. "We'll get as far as we can first. The structure in the front left corner is the weapons shed?" He saw Reynolds nod in the shadows. "What about the middle structure? The big one?"

"Barracks. Captain sleeps in the small building to its right."

Cael thought for a split second. It was demoralizing to a unit to lose their commander. And it could send the rebels into disarray. But he was one man. They needed to get rid of as many as possible.

"If this thing turns into a goat screw, take out the barracks. I'll take the weapons shed." In a perfect world they'd release the other prisoners and make their way undetected out of the camp. Some distance away he'd call for military backup and let the choppers provide aerial firepower to take out the camp.

He'd never encountered a perfect world yet.

"Carter's out there providing cover for us." He belly-crawled around the cells, divested the two guards of their weapons and crawled back, handing one extra rifle to Reynolds. "For Perez." He took a moment to sit propped up against a cell next to his friend, and looked at him. "Let's do this."

He took the first cell, unhooked the door and ducked in. De la Reyes was slumped inside. He barely stirred at his entrance. There was no time to check on his injuries. Cael got down and lifted the man's arm around his neck so he could support him and rose again, swiftly exiting the cell. He saw Reynolds give a rifle to Perez, and signal the unknown man to follow them.

The stranger ran in a crouch toward Cael. "Give me a weapon," he whispered.

"Not a chance." Without knowing exactly who they were dealing with, there was no way he was going to trust him. Instead, he had the man support the president, who seemed only half conscious. "Keep down and stay with us."

He led the way, all of them staying low to avoid detection. When he got to the trip wires he signaled the group behind him of their location. The booby traps he'd dismantled earlier on recon.

As a matter of fact, the lack of problems was almost eerie.

He'd no sooner had the thought than he heard the faint pop of Ava's silencer. Turning to look behind him, he saw the body of another perimeter sentry crumple.

In the next moment all hell broke loose.

Automatic gunfire sounded. The sentry posted on the front corner perimeter closest to them had opened fire on Ava. Cael saw her hit the ground. Saw the bullet spray kick up mud all around her. His heart stopped.

He returned fire on the sentry, just before Ava's rifle sounded again. And a crazy fireball of hope spiraled inside him. "Go, go, go!" Cael waved the others by. He ran in a crouch to Ava's side, aware that the camp was coming to life behind him.

"Are you hit?" He ran his free hand frantically over her body, barely registering her answer.

"I'm fine."

"Then move!" He nudged her after the others and turned to find Reynolds alongside him. Each of them pulled the pins of the grenades and heaved them high.

Soldiers were pouring out of the barracks. Some were already returning fire. He and Reynolds turned and ran, staying low with hands over their ears, wanting to put as much distance between them and the camp as possible.

Seconds later the grenades exploded and turned the night to flame.

It was a motley looking crew in on the debriefing, Cael noted, gazing around the table. De la Reyes swayed slightly as he sat at the head of the table, his physician hovering around him, trying to conduct a thorough examination. Quintero sat at his side, casting worried glances at the president.

As for the rest of them…Ava and Reynolds still wore blackening on their faces, as he did himself. Perez's face was swollen and bruised, although he wasn't in as bad a shape as de la Reyes. And the stranger they'd rescued looked gaunt, as if he'd been starved for a time. There were fresh-looking scars, healing badly, marring his hands and face.

Cael looked at Ava. "Tell the doctor when he finishes with the president to look at him." He jerked his head toward the stranger. He waited for her to translate before adding, "Then he can check you out."

She lifted a brow coolly. "I'm fine."

"Damn straight," murmured Reynolds, earning himself a quick look from Cael. The man shrugged. "Dangerous women. It's a weakness, like I said."

Apparently it was a weakness they shared.

"You took an unnecessary risk with the president's life," Quintero said imperiously. "You should have used the militia earlier for the rescue."

It was a moment before Cael could shift his attention away from Ava. He wouldn't be satisfied she was all right until he could check for himself, going over every inch of that exquisite skin again, inch by inch.

But for the time being, he had to deal with the matter at hand. "I wasn't going to divulge the coordinates until after we were out of there. I couldn't risk them coming in too soon and catching us in the cross fire." And he hadn't wanted to chance going in with ground units he wasn't sure he could trust. But he knew better than to say that.

"That is ridiculous. Our military is highly trained. They could have—"

"Enough, Ernesto." Although he was looking much the worse for wear, the president's voice was authoritative. "Senor McCabe executed the rescue mission flawlessly. And our military handily provided some aerial firepower that helped us leave our pursuers behind."

It was an abbreviated explanation for their escape, Cael conceded silently. The choppers hadn't arrived for well over a half hour after they'd detonated the camp. A harrowing half hour in which they'd had to make their way to freedom hauling injured prisoners while returning fire against the rebels chasing them.

The president looked at him. "My military commander reported that they rounded up nearly seventy rebels who were not killed in the blast. The police picked up Miss Fuente and her driver. They are in custody."

Cael had a moment to wonder if the regret in the man's voice was for the woman's fate, or for placing them all at risk by trusting her in the first place. It was doubtful the man would be nearly as trusting of the next female he became involved with.

"Tell us about the demands Ramirez made. You didn't release his assets?"

Quintero shook his head in response to the president's question. "We drew out the process, as Miss Carter suggested. Pretended there was much bureaucracy to cut through." He looked at Ava. "The green tape you mentioned."

Ava gave the man a slight smile. "Red tape. But yeah. That was exactly right."

Cael glanced back at de la Reyes. "We need to check with Justice. Ramirez will be forced to make a move soon. With his assets frozen and your escape, he's out of options. You might also want to put heavy security on the airport, borders and harbors for the time being."

The president nodded. "I will put the call in right away."

"I'd hesitate to include the local police force in any final plans for his capture," Reynolds put in bluntly. "I went to them when I was looking for Perez. Talked to some of the policemen involved in the interrogation of the airport dispatcher. I was approached by a uniform in town an hour later, saying they had information about Perez's whereabouts." He glanced at the silent operative. "Got blindsided. Knocked me over the head and threw me in the back of a truck. Drove me to the edge of the jungle and handed me over to the rebels."

"Carbon copy," muttered Perez. "They grabbed me up about an hour after the interrogation ended. Claimed there was a break in the case and they were to take me back to the headquarters."

The look on de la Reyes's face was thunderous. "You can identify these men?"

The two nodded.

"This, too, will be dealt with immediately. There is disloyalty all around us." There was a flash across his expression, and Cael knew he was thinking of the woman who had betrayed them. "Each of these untrustworthy individuals put lives at risk. And they will be dealt with harshly."

Cael's gaze went to the stranger sitting at the table who had been listening silently. It remained to be seen whether the man would end up in a San Baltes prison or be sent back to the States. "You're up, Jonny. What's your story?"

The man had been sitting back, taking it all in. And Cael knew he'd been as distrustful of his "rescuers" as they had of him. "Jonny Streich, NSWU-Eight."

Cael straightened, narrowed his eyes at the man. "Son of a bitch," he murmured. Without looking at him, he knew Reynolds was just as alert.

Although American law prohibits the country's military from active combat in allied countries, there were quiet deployments to support the antidrug efforts in South American countries. The Naval Special Warfare Unit Eight was one of those teams. Their task was to provide Mobile Training Teams to train the South American host personnel.

Like most South American countries, San Baltes had an extensive river system. Ramirez, along with a lot of his drug dealer counterparts in neighboring countries, used the rivers as a highway for his drugs.

"Another U.S. Special Boat Squadron member and I were assigned to military boat twenty-seven. We were ambushed and overrun by rebels ten days ago. Those who weren't killed in the battle were taken prisoner." He looked at de la Reyes. "I regret to inform you, sir, that your military personnel who were captured were killed in captivity."

Cael exchanged a look with Ava. That explained the pile of bodies they'd discovered at the deserted camp.

De la Reyes swallowed, gave a slow nod. "I had heard of the ambush while I was in the States. I want to thank you for your service." His gaze found Cael's. "And I owe a debt of gratitude to you, Senor McCabe, and your team that cannot be repaid. Anything that I can do for you, anything at all, you have but to ask."

But Cael's mind had started working the first moment

Streich had explained his presence there. His gaze landed thoughtfully on Ava, while he answered, "As a matter of fact, President de la Reyes, there is one thing…."

The first hint Ava had that she wasn't alone in the bathroom was when the shower door opened. She whirled around, found her defensive blow deflected when Cael caught her wrist in one of his hands.

The man was silent as a snake, she fumed. Twisting free, she asked truculently, "What are you doing in here?"

"I'm dirty," was his innocent reply. She watched, her ire splintering, as he stripped swiftly. It wasn't fair, she reflected dimly, that the sight of all that bare skin over bulging muscle and sinew should turn her bones to mush.

"You have a shower in your room," she pointed out as he crowded in with her. Immediately the stall grew smaller. She felt surrounded by the breadth of him. Felt the kick start to her pulse as her body responded accordingly.

"But yours was already running." He leaned in then and, guessing his intent, Ava dodged around him, nudging him under the spray.

"Like you said, you're dirty."

He reached out a hand to snag her wrist, ensuring that she didn't go too far while he washed the mud and grime away. And Ava was content to remain in place.

The rest of his team would be flying in tomorrow and her time here would be through. The thought brought a cold bolt of dread that she strove to shake off. She had plenty of regrets over choices she'd made in the past, choices that she was going to have to answer for when she got home to her son.

But she wouldn't regret the time spent with Cael McCabe.

"What were you talking about with the president after the rest of us left?" She'd noted his thoughtful gaze on her before he'd answered de la Reyes at the end. Didn't much appreciate not being in on the conversation if it pertained to her.

"Believe it or not, I've got a plan." His voice was muffled since he was scrubbing his face with her washcloth.

"There's a news flash."

She dodged his fingers when he released her for a quick retaliatory pinch, and took the soap, running it over the broad expanse of his shoulders. There was power there, in the muscles that jumped and worked beneath her fingers as she smoothed her soapy palms over his back. A strength that was all the more devastating when it was tempered by tenderness.

Just the memory had heat flooding her belly. She'd promised herself she wouldn't indulge in regrets, so she'd tuck the memories away for the future when memories were all she had. But her touch slowed purposely to savor the tactile sensation beneath her fingertips. It'd be one more image to add to her mental scrapbook and she was fiercely determined that their parting be unmarred by remorse. Of any kind.

When he turned to her his face was clean, save for the day's growth of whiskers. They made him look tougher somehow. A bit uncivilized. She raised a hand to brush his stubbled jaw with her palm. He slid an arm around her waist to pull her closer.

"Normally I like to keep details of my security missions under wraps, for a host of reasons. But this time I've asked de la Reyes to make some phone calls on our behalf."

She stopped midstroke. "What kind of calls? To whom?"

"To the Pentagon, for starters. He'll verify Streich's identity and then he'll be talking to everyone he can contact, both there and in the White House, to sing our praises for the rescue of both him and a U.S. military officer." He made a slight grimace, as if the thought embarrassed him a bit. "Like I say, not my usual thing. When the national media get hold of it later in the day it's going to be a free-for-all. So I'm going to arrange for private transport to fly you back and to get you from the airport. You might want to plan for you and your son to stay elsewhere for a few days. I'm guessing reporters will be camped on your doorstep."

The desolation that pooled in her stomach at his easy talk of her departure was alarming. She couldn't afford to react emotionally. Not now, when there was so much at stake. Protecting Alex had to be her first concern and there were a few details missing from his "plan."

"And what is all this supposed to accomplish?"

His grin was roguish. "It's called deflection, baby. And it's a preemptive strike that will make it politically impossible for Samuelson to strong-arm you. Even if he did expose your parentage to the public or to your superiors, your heroic stature is going to make you untouchable. If anything, the news stories will just shift to contrast your character with your father's. Not exactly pleasant, I admit," he added, when she made a face. "But you still come out of it undamaged, with your reputation and your career intact."

He free hand slid up to cup her breast, toy with the nipple. He was, she thought, with a hitch of her breath, a bit too easily sidetracked.

"And what about you?"

One broad shoulder lifted. "Basically the same thing. Timing won't be the best for the smear campaign I assume he has planned. He'll have to wait until the next opportunity arises. It'll drive the son of a bitch crazy."

She eyed him knowingly. "But it won't help you destroy him."

The humor abruptly fled from his expression. He shifted so the water continued to cascade over his shoulders, making little rivulets over his arms and chest. "No. It recently came to my attention that there might be more important things to concentrate on than to one-up my biological father."

There was a jitter in her pulse. His green eyes were alight with an emotion that she couldn't identify. Was afraid to identify. But it sparked spurts of answering heat in her veins.

"And when did this moment of enlightenment occur?"

His arm around her waist tightened. "Might've been when I saw you standing there providing cover for us, as bullets kicked up the dirt all around you. But it started before that. I just didn't realize what the hell had me so distracted where you were concerned."

Her feminine smile of satisfaction curled her lips. "Her distraction, was I?" Linking her arms around his neck, she nipped the side of his throat ungently. "I didn't notice that you were particularly diverted when you were threatening me."

"I should have been tipped off when I became more concerned with protecting you from Samuelson than I was in destroying the prick for good," he murmured, tipping her chin up to brush her lips with his. "As it is, you played hell with my intentions, because I became more worried about protecting you than getting the best of him. I don't have a whole lot of experience in the area, but I figure that means I'm crazy in love with you."

Her heart did a slow, lazy spin in her chest. "I'm not going to quibble with your definition. Especially since I haven't been able to get you out of my head since we first met. I love you—" The rest of her words were lost when his mouth came down more firmly on hers. Her fingers curled into his hair as little thrills of pleasure skipped up her spine.

By the time he lifted his head, her thoughts had scattered. "This is going to be complicated," she said faintly as he scored her earlobe with his teeth.

"Simple," he disputed, his mouth busy. "Very, very simple."

She tried to gather her fragmented logic. "Our jobs…I can't move. I wouldn't do that to Alex. He has three more years of high school."

He leaned back to smile at her then, as he skated a possessive hand down her back. "Don't worry about a thing. I'll make a plan."

Epilogue

The wedding organist was just beginning to play when Dace Recker stepped out to stand alone at the altar, looking decidedly more jittery than he did on an incident response. A moment later, Cael and Alex joined Ava in the pew. She sent Cael a reproving look, but he just winked at her. "We got stuck in traffic," he whispered loudly.

Beyond him, Alex grinned. "Yeah, traffic."

She lifted a brow to indicate she didn't for a second believe either of them. Unless traffic was the latest euphemism for extra batting practice these days.

But it was hard to be annoyed when she saw daily how well her son got along with the man she loved. And she and Alex were back on an even keel now, although there'd been some rocky days when she'd first returned from San Baltes. He'd been accusing and disappointed by turns, and she'd accepted the blame for not being honest with him about his grandfather. He'd deserved to know the truth at some point, although God help her, if this hadn't happened she still didn't know when that point would have come. It was difficult to balance her son's right to know with her overwhelming need to protect him.

But the more Alex had read about Calvin Julson, the more he'd understood her reticence on the subject. And the more his ire had faded. The man's past was ugly enough to dim any burgeoning thoughts of long-lost reunions. And that was a disappointment she couldn't shield him against.

Lindsay Bradford and Jack Langley walked up the aisle arm in arm. As maid of honor and best man respectively, they would be the only attendants in the wedding. And judging from the rock on Lindsay's finger, Ava would be attending another wedding sometime in the near future.

She gave a slight shake of her head. It was difficult to imagine Langley, the dark-haired charmer with the devilish grin, as marriage material, but judging from the way he was looking at Lindsay, he'd finally met his match.

The music changed, and Ava turned to see her friend Jolie Conrad walking down the aisle. There was a dizzying sense of bemusement at all the changes that had taken place in the last few months for some of the members on the Alpha Squad.

Cael's hand slipped into hers and their fingers interlocked as Ava turned to smile at him. It seemed fitting somehow that this man was at her side as she watched her friends begin their future together.

Because whatever the future had in store for her, she knew Cael was going to be part of it.

* * * * *

Celebrate 60 years of pure reading pleasure with Harlequin!

To commemorate the event, Harlequin Intrigue® is thrilled to invite you to the wedding of The Colby Agency's J. T. Baxley and his bride, Eve Mattson.

That is, of course, if J.T. can find the woman who left him at the altar. Considering he's a private investigator for one of the top agencies in the country—the best of the best—that shouldn't be a problem. The real setback is that his bride isn't who she appears to be…and her mysterious past has put them both in danger.

Enjoy an exclusive glimpse of Debra Webb's latest addition to
THE COLBY AGENCY:
ELITE RECONNAISSANCE DIVISION

THE BRIDE'S SECRETS

Available August 2009 from Harlequin Intrigue®.

The dark figures on the dock were still firing. The bullets cutting through the surface of the water without the warning boom of shots told Eve they were using silencers.

That was to her benefit. Silencers decreased the accuracy of every shot and lessened the range.

She grabbed for the rocks. Scrambled through the darkness. Bumped her knee on a boulder. Cursed.

Burrowing into the waist-deep grass, she kept low and crawled forward. Faster. Pushed harder. Needed as much distance as possible.

Shots pinged on the rocks.

J.T. scrambled alongside her.

He was breathing hard.

They had to stay close to the ground until they reached the next row of warehouses. Even though she was relatively certain they were out of range at this point, she wasn't taking any risks. And she wasn't slowing down.

J.T. had to keep up.

The splat of a bullet hitting the ground next to Eve had her rolling left. Maybe they weren't completely out of range.

She bumped J.T. He grunted.

His injured arm. Dammit. She could apologize later.

Half a dozen more yards.

Almost in the clear.

As she reached the cover of the alley between the first two warehouses she tensed.

Silence.

No pings or splats.

She glanced back at the dock. Deserted.

Time to run.

Her car was parked another block down.

Pushing to her feet, she sprinted forward. The wet bag dragged at her shoulder. She ignored it.

By the time she reached the lot where her car was parked, she had dug the keys from her pocket and hit the fob. Six seconds later she was behind the wheel. She hit the ignition as J.T. collapsed into the passenger seat. Tires squealed as she spun out of the slot.

"What the hell did you do to me?"

From the corner of her eye she watched him shake his head in an attempt to clear it.

He would be pissed when she told him about the tranquilizer. She'd needed him cooperative until she formulated a plan. A drug-induced state of unconsciousness had been the fastest and most efficient method to ensure his continued solidarity.

"I can't really talk right now." Eve weaved into the right lane as the street widened to four lanes. What she needed was traffic. It was Saturday night—shouldn't be that difficult to find as soon as they were out of the old warehouse district.

A glance in the rearview mirror warned that their unwanted company had caught up.

Sensing her tension, J.T. turned to peer over his left shoulder.

"I hope you have a plan B."

She shot him a look. "There's always plan G." Then she pulled the Glock out of her waistband.

Cutting the steering wheel left, she slid between two vehicles. Another veer to the right and she'd put several cars between hers and the enemy.

She was betting they wouldn't pull out the firepower in the open like this, but a girl could never be too sure when it came to an unknown enemy.

Deep blending was the way to go.

Two traffic lights ahead the marquis of a movie theater provided exactly the opportunity she was looking for.

The digital numbers on the dash indicated it was just past midnight. Perfect timing. The late movie would be purging its audience into the crowd of teenagers who liked hanging out in the parking lot.

She took a hard right onto the property that sported a twelve-screen theater, numerous fast-food hot spots and a chain superstore. Speeding across the lot, she selected a lane of parking slots. Pulling in as close to the theater entrance as possible, she shut off the engine and reached for her door.

"Let's go."

Thankfully he didn't argue.

Rounding the hood of her car, she shoved the Glock into her bag, then wrapped her arm around J.T.'s and merged into the crowd.

With her free hand she finger-combed her long hair. It was soaked, as were her clothes. The kids she bumped into noticed, gave her death-ray glares.

They just didn't know.

As she and J.T. moved in closer to the building, she grabbed a baseball cap from an innocent bystander. The crowd made it easy. The kid who owned the cap had made it even easier by stuffing the cap bill-first into his waistband at the small of his back.

Pushing through the loitering crowd, she made her way to the side of the building next to the main entrance. She pushed J.T. against the wall and dropped her bag to the ground. Peeled off her tee and let it fall.

His gaze instantly zeroed in on her breasts, where the cami she wore had glued to her skin like an extra layer. A zing of desire shot through her veins.

Not the time.

With a flick of her wrist she twisted her hair up and clamped the cap atop the blonde mass.

"They're coming," J.T. muttered as he gazed at some point beyond her.

"Yeah, I know." She planted her palms against the wall on either side of him and leaned in. "Keep your eyes open. Let me know when they're inside."

Then she planted her lips on his.

* * * * *

Will J.T. and Eve be caught in the moment?
Or will Eve get the chance to reveal all of her secrets?
Find out in
THE BRIDE'S SECRETS
by Debra Webb
Available August 2009 from Harlequin Intrigue®

We'll be spotlighting a different series every month throughout 2009 to celebrate our 60th anniversary.

LOOK FOR
HARLEQUIN INTRIGUE®
IN AUGUST!

To commemorate the event, Harlequin Intrigue® is thrilled to invite you to the wedding of the Colby Agency's J. T. Baxley and his bride, Eve Mattson.

Look for *Colby Agency: Elite Reconnaissance*

THE BRIDE'S SECRETS
BY DEBRA WEBB

Available August 2009

www.eHarlequin.com

HIBPA09

You're invited to join our Tell Harlequin Reader Panel!

By joining our new reader panel you will:

- Receive Harlequin® books—they are FREE and yours to keep with no obligation to purchase anything!
- Participate in fun online surveys
- Exchange opinions and ideas with women just like you
- Have a say in our new book ideas and help us publish the best in women's fiction

In addition, you will have a chance to win great prizes and receive special gifts! See Web site for details. Some conditions apply. Space is limited.

To join, visit us at
www.TellHarlequin.com.

REQUEST YOUR FREE BOOKS!

2 FREE NOVELS PLUS 2 FREE GIFTS!

Silhouette® Romantic

SUSPENSE

Sparked by Danger, Fueled by Passion!

YES! Please send me 2 FREE Silhouette® Romantic Suspense novels and my 2 FREE gifts (gifts are worth about $10). After receiving them, if I don't wish to receive any more books, I can return the shipping statement marked "cancel." If I don't cancel, I will receive 4 brand-new novels every month and be billed just $4.24 per book in the U.S. or $4.99 per book in Canada. That's a savings of at least 15% off the cover price! It's quite a bargain! Shipping and handling is just 50¢ per book*. I understand that accepting the 2 free books and gifts places me under no obligation to buy anything. I can always return a shipment and cancel at any time. Even if I never buy another book from Silhouette, the two free books and gifts are mine to keep forever.

240 SDN EYL4 340 SDN EYMG

Name _____ (PLEASE PRINT) _____

Address _____ Apt. # _____

City _____ State/Prov. _____ Zip/Postal Code _____

Signature (if under 18, a parent or guardian must sign) _____

Mail to the Silhouette Reader Service:

IN U.S.A.: P.O. Box 1867, Buffalo, NY 14240-1867
IN CANADA: P.O. Box 609, Fort Erie, Ontario L2A 5X3

Not valid to current subscribers of Silhouette Romantic Suspense books.

Want to try two free books from another line?
Call 1-800-873-8635 or visit www.morefreebooks.com.

* Terms and prices subject to change without notice. Prices do not include applicable taxes. Sales tax applicable in N.Y. Canadian residents will be charged applicable provincial taxes and GST. Offer not valid in Quebec. This offer is limited to one order per household. All orders subject to approval. Credit or debit balances in a customer's account(s) may be offset by any other outstanding balance owed by or to the customer. Please allow 4 to 6 weeks for delivery. Offer available while quantities last.

Your Privacy: Silhouette is committed to protecting your privacy. Our Privacy Policy is available online at www.eHarlequin.com or upon request from the Reader Service. From time to time we make our lists of customers available to reputable third parties who may have a product or service of interest to you. If you would prefer we not share your name and address, please check here. ☐

SRS09R

Stay up-to-date on all your romance reading news!

HARLEQUIN free

Inside ROMANCE

APRIL | MAY | JUNE 2009

CELEBRATE 60 YEARS
OF PURE READING PLEASURE
WITH MORE EXCITING SERIES
SPOTLIGHTS, FEATURED
EVERY MONTH!

NEW YORK TIMES
BESTSELLING AUTHOR
DIANA PALMER
BRINGS YOU A
BRAND-NEW STORY!

CELEBRATE
MOTHER'S DAY
WITH HARLEQUIN®!

60   HARLEQUIN   Silhouette

The Harlequin
Inside Romance
newsletter is a **FREE**
quarterly newsletter
highlighting
our upcoming
series releases
and promotions!

Go to
eHarlequin.com/InsideRomance
or e-mail us at
InsideRomance@Harlequin.com
to sign up to receive
your **FREE** newsletter today!

In 2009 Harlequin celebrates
60 years of pure reading pleasure!

We're marking this occasion by offering
16 **FREE** full books to download and read.

We invite you to visit and share the Web site
with your friends, family
and anyone who enjoys reading.

Silhouette®
Romantic
SUSPENSE

COMING NEXT MONTH

Available July 28, 2009

#1571 CAVANAUGH PRIDE—Marie Ferrarella
Cavanaugh Justice
When detective Julianne White Bear is sent from another town to help hunt a serial killer, she brings with her a secret motive. Detective Frank McIntyre has his hands full heading the task force, but he can't deny his attraction toward Julianne—and the feeling is mutual. They're determined to put romance on hold until justice is served, but it isn't always that easy....

#1572 HER 24-HOUR PROTECTOR—Loreth Anne White
Love in 60 Seconds
FBI agent Lex Duncan and casino heiress Jenna Rothchild play each other from the moment they meet. Even as the heat between the two sizzles hotter than the Las Vegas desert, danger intensifies around them. Suddenly Lex becomes the one man who can rescue the sexy young heiress…in more ways than one.

#1573 HIS PERSONAL MISSION—Justine Davis
Redstone, Incorporated
Ryan Barton's teenage sister is missing, and his only hope to find her is Sasha Tereschenko—the woman he'd loved and lost two years ago. Family is everything to Sasha, who leaps into action. While the two track down the predator possibly holding Ryan's sister, their former attraction arises again, and their lives—and hearts—are put at risk.

#1574 SILENT WATCH—Elle Kennedy
Samantha Dawson has been in hiding since the night of her brutal attack. Now, living in isolation under a new identity, she is surprised to find a sexy FBI agent on her doorstep. Blake Corwin promises to protect Samantha in exchange for her help with her attacker's latest victim. But the last thing he expected was to fall for Sam, and when she again becomes a target, Blake will do anything to save her.

SRSCNMBPA0709